# WE MUST SAVE JEPSON!

## MARK PETERSEN

Published in the United States of America by Dunmore Books.
Interior Design by Ampersand Book Interiors
Cover Design by The Thatchery
Map image courtesy of antiqueprints.com

First Printing, 2020

ISBN 978-1-7350631-0-2

# LETTER I.

*(Extracts from a letter written by Mr. H. R. Huxtable to the Honourable Chairman of the Royal Order of the Muskrat's Jepson Relief Committee, dated from the steamer* Charity, *River Bambesi, Africa, 1 April 1888)*

Murchison—

Salutations from the End of the World. Or thereabouts. Huzzah, huzzah, England! How are you, old dog? At present a gauzy mist envelopes us. Having for the most part successfully been fitted out, we steam up the Bambesi's mouth from the West Coast like so many pilgrim phantoms. Our ship lists, working its way past Cassava Point.

To my chagrin, our gin-soaked pilot, Hendricke, lists, too. A mysterious figure in his ragged robe and turban snatched from one of our Zanzibaris, he staggers about his teakwood deck-house. The Bambesi presents a deep channel here. Yet more than once we have been run aground by sand and his stupidity.

Recently, when I planted the Union Jack at his leaky craft's bow, in his fog the river-rat smirked and whizzed an emptied gin bottle by my head. Apparently he is a man not much for moral elevation.

"Spare the rod, use the whip," he said.

I pushed back my hair and frowned at him.

"Or the gin bottle."

He grunted, then waved a hand.

"Out there? You'll not last a week, not one week."

Yesterday the brute overran and nearly killed a native fisherman trying to cast a net into the waters before us. Afterwards, he banged on a leaky steam pipe and wrapped it with his turban. His lips drooped, showing only stumps of teeth.

"The whip," he said to no one in particular. "The bloody whip."

To compound my chagrin, the fellow makes good company for my equally intemperate captains, Percy Fuggleby and Francis Muffin. Veritable priests of Bacchus, they promise to go down drinking. Captain Fuggleby is irritable enough when sober; nor is Muffin the Crown's finest representative. Perhaps it is the heat. They may also resent serving under a librarian with no military or adventuring experience.

Given their uncivil natures, I suspect they are on this mission to avoid prison sentences—or even to dodge the noose. They may also have been pulled up out of a gutter. Still, I suspect they would be assets in a pub punch-up.

Taking on their help seems like thrusting a bullet into a revolver and spinning it, but I have few options.

There is much to learn here. Right away I realised my black tailcoat was impractical. My cotton tunic suffices. I failed to don my sun helmet the other day, and presently my skin is lobster-pink. As to boating, I am afraid I would not know a starboard if one hit me on the head.

Regarding land travel hereabouts, I am mindful of the advice imparted by my nearly talented colleague, J. Scott Keltie, Librarian to the Royal Geographic Society:

"Day after day you toil through the frightful, unending cobweb of the pathless forest, hacking your way amid the gloomy twilight of the giant trees through a black snaky tangle of matted boughs and tough, wiry creepers and huge dagger-like thorns, while the damp, foul, steaming vapour makes your head sick and your limbs faint, and you feel your strength failing hour by hour…"

(Insert, Honourable Chairman, some fierce savages and toothy crocodiles, and you get the rest of Mr. Keltie's picture.)

This description does not cheer me. Despite Mr. Keltie's alleged robust exploits, though, I doubt whether he has ever even traversed the Channel, let alone the Dark Continent. We librarians—a cerebral tribe not known for adventuring—would seem to share active imaginations. I suppose the man may have fallen down a ravine once somewhere.

After glancing over my shoulder and reading this passage from Keltie's preface to "Letters of Stanley," our surgeon has abandoned ship, bound perhaps for the fleshpots of Egypt. I wish he had taken the rats and roaches with him.

This did not feel auspicious, and unfortunately Muffin and Fuggleby have taken to his medicinal comforts with gusto.

Did I mention the heat?

And, speaking of same, did I mention Miss Eaton of the Christians for Celibacy Society? When I first met her, she screeched on about superstition's dominion and the light of Christianity. Yet I suspect she has baser motives for journeying with us: she is the sole member of the feminine persuasion to accompany our party of nigh 200 half-clothed men into the steamy depths of this untamed region.

The other day, she gave me a smutty smile. All sharp nose and brunette curls, she tried to explain her presence.

"'uman depravity, like the malice of Satan, 'as worn its darkest scowl among the loveliest scenes."

Beyond a bend in the river rose lumpy and flat-topped hills. I blew out a breath. "Miss Eaton, I trust you will not unduly excite the men."

Heedless of my point, she whispered back: "Use the whip."

Our carriers are a tall, good-natured lot, and do not want trouble; they keep their distance from her. On the other hand, Virgil, my diminutive loin-clothed Wambutti guide and interpreter, has taken a liking to her. He regularly begs her to accompany his fiddling with her foghorn soprano. Now and then the mist rises and the carriers joke that the locals we spot beaching their canoes and dashing into the mangroves do so not for fear of being enslaved, but in response to the wailing duo.

Apparently these natives—seeing evil spirits everywhere—fancy the *Charity* a floating apparition.

We come upon their stilt-mounted huts hidden away in bowers of coconut palms. One good screech of our vessel's whistle keeps them at a distance.

Still, a short while ago Captain Fuggleby yelled rudely toward the shores.

"Run! Hide! Bugger off!"

"That's enough, Fuggleby," I said.

The man is ruddy of face and ruby-nosed. In response, he brushed thoughtfully at his moustache, which tapers to long tips. His sleeves were rolled up, revealing stout forearms. He made a scoffing sound.

"My, my, my. A fine man, ain't you?"

Bold leader that I intend to be, I stared back.

"And you're dangerously close to impertinence." I heaved a sigh fruity with disgust. "The hellish nerve you have. Consider this an area for improvement, sir! Have a good think."

He grinned rabidly at me.

I said, a little louder, "You understand, Captain?"

Again he said nothing. So I thrust my face forward.

"Captain?"

He spat a dark stream of tobacco juice onto the deck.

"Oh my," he said at last.

The brute refers to the locals as "black demons." He claims he would be happy to shoot them without provocation. Just who, then, is the demon?

Howling all the while like a whirling dervish, Virgil plays his one-stringed fiddle incessantly. Even without Miss Eaton, the noise is dreadful. The tiny bloke is a sight to behold: beardless, with two brass earrings, all sinew and muscle, sepia skin, and vivid, knowing eyes.

In his broken English, he tells me wild stories about men with horns on their heads as he fingers his monkey-teeth necklace. A clever and industrious fellow, he practices with his long blowgun daily.

He has taken to smoking a pipe like me, and together we fill the air with a rich, hickory aroma. The fellow served under Colonel Sneath prior, and carries many languages under his belt. As well as English, he is versed in the major African vernaculars.

As I write, rocking gently with the deck's motion, the carriers snicker yet at my good-luck scarf and cracked eyeglasses. My nose peels, and I have been gripped by a violent diarrhoea. No matter what happens, though, I will not waver. Our force will reach Central Africa and save Jepson and his desert wilderness post.

Providence willing, perhaps we will even sight the rare albino African muskrat.

Once I lay down my ink-pen, I will revel in the breeze on my cheek as our vessel steams along. We have a clearing of the mist now. Ahead swirl the white waters of rapids. Herons stalk through the shallows alongside us. An unbroken screen of green edges the riverbanks, and amidships the funnel smokes and roars.

Miss Eaton sits like Cleopatra in the bow.

Bowl of boiled green bananas in hand, Virgil has stepped up to my side.

"Miss Eaton hopes you to join her when you finish."

"Unlikely. No, out of the question."

"But—"

"How do I put this?" I drew on my pipe and stared at his pleasant face, then cleared my throat. "I dare say the throbbing engines may be exciting her nether regions."

I could not decipher the look he gave me.

Well, give my regards to our fellow lodge members and other subscribers of the Relief Fund, Murchison. Hip, hip, hooray. Science, progress, and all that.

I will sign off now. I suspect great suffering may await us. For now, my tea is cooling.

Your obedient servant,

H. R. Huxtable, Expedition Leader

# LETTER II.

*(Addressed to Mrs. H. R. Huxtable, dated 4 April 1886, from somewhere on the Bambesi River)*

Dear Mother—

Considering the dangers ahead, our force may lay down the knife and fork for good ourselves; yet I must admit I hope Aunt Edna hangs. Resting here in my hammock, I cannot help but wonder how she fared in court. (Poor Uncle Uriah—have they found the body yet? But I imagine the authorities would not choose to drag the Thames.) She should never have asked you in your fragile condition to testify on her behalf.

How are you and venerable Papa? Despite being entered on St. Helene's Church's birth register as "Hubert Reginald Huxtable, Bastard," I am forever thankful for all you both have done for me. You are a good mother and I love you.

We lead a rugged existence here in the tropic wilds: I have muddied my new breeches already. As I practiced my donkey-riding on deck yesterday, the beast suddenly bolted across the aft (?) deck. I tipped over his shoulder and pitched (rather like Uncle Uriah, I surmise) right over the *Charity*'s side and into the water. This proved amusing to all except me. I suspect my guide Virgil and his blowgun were involved, as not all his darts are tipped with poison. Fortunately, no ravenous crocodiles lurked about and I was fished safely from the river.

Some items—poetic, factual, and otherwise—for your drawing-room perusal:

I have seen many a yawning hippo lazing on white sandbars. The creatures bear a striking likeness to Aunt Edna.

We may soon have to abandon our vessel, which in any case reeks of sweat, wood smoke, and salted fish. In the faster water of our easterly course, we seem to float in a rudderless tea-pot. Our helmsman is a hopeless dipsomaniac, and the steamer itself is apparently plagued with an ailing furnace and myriad leaks. She lists markedly. Both man and boat seem to have a propensity for hitting shoals and sunken rocks. Presently we puff along slowly in a rather asthmatic fashion.

"I hope Fort Bim can hold," I said to our pilot in the wheelhouse only minutes ago.

Black clouds huddled in the distance as he rolled his bleary eyes. His face ran with sweat, and his disagreeable breath smelled of cheap port.

"The rats ain't jumped ship yet. But your march into the jungle?"

"We will be—"

"Crackers!" He squinted downriver, spun the boat's wheel, and cackled. "Think you can manage it? Think that, you got a sickness."

"Rubbish."

Long native arrows lodge in his pilot house, Mother. He leaves them there with an eerie sort of pride. We are now some 6,000 miles from London, he assures me.

I think of Lord Beaconsfield's words: "Adventures are for the adventurous."

The river waits like a silver snake.

Have you ever smoked a pipe, Mother? No, maybe not. There is something to them. They lend a patriarchal air to my ways, I fancy.

Did I mention the heat? At times it hits one like a club.

On the advice of our recently disappeared doctor, I have been taking a nasty cure for my general ailments: a concoction of boiled bottled seawater and goat's milk. The medicine may be worse than the illness.

A famine disrupts the regions we will traverse, or so says the Arab trader we recently met. Loins wound round with rags, the man exchanged salaams and took hold of our sounding-pole from a dugout loaded with ivory and savage paddlers. Hendricke, our pilot, soon made great sport of splashing them with our vessel's stern-wheel.

The heat brings out the brute and mischief in us, I think. "Let not Satan prevail over me, my Lord Jesus," I pray nightly.

Do you know the Eatons from the West End, Mother? They are less than prim, I imagine. Our sole female companion is of them, and I suspect her family spends most of its time in beer houses and gin palaces.

Excuse me a moment while I dab my brow with a handkerchief. Just now I glimpse a small bird flitting into a crocodile's mouth and picking its teeth—somehow the sight perturbs me.

When opportunity presents, I practice with my Winchester. The Good Shepherd deserts not his flock when wolves come.

Virgil tells me of local customs, their rude ideas of justice and wisdom. For instance, there is a convention known as the "wife price." If a husband mistreats his betrothed, or is a no-good, she may simply return to her family. If she is a no-good herself, he gets compensation back.

I figure Uncle Uriah's family (may he rest in eternal peace) is due for a full refund.

Virgil calls me "Mukungu" (White Man).

"There's a dignified sound to that," I told him. "Rest assured, soon we're going to astonish the world. And astonish ourselves."

He is a fine companion. His cheeriness endears him to all.

Mother, I do miss your pigeon pie and Yorkshire pudding. Oh yes, enclosed is a cowrie-shell necklace for your and Father's titillation. I imagine you pray that I do not end up simmering in some cannibal's dinner-pot. Do not worry.

Still, who knows which way the brazen dice of fate will fall? The native drums we hear so often along our course may not bode well for the future.

"Our route?" Virgil tells me. "It will be risky."

Your loving son,<br>Hubert

# LETTER III.

*(From H. R. Huxtable to Goldsworthy Jepson, Governour, from the upper Bambesi, ? April 1888)*

Dear Sir—

I trust you and your troops hold on yet. Given our great empire's present involvement in copious conflicts, we have assembled a volunteer force to bring you relief. Take heart: ammunition and general assistance are on the way. If we push, we will reach you by July.

We have word of famine and belligerent tribes along our intended route. We also hear that, besides the threat of the Mahdi and his Arab forces which you face, the Troops of the Equatorial Province are ready to break allegiance and revolt.

As to any surly tribes in our own path, we will throw bright beads at them. Or we will brandish our rifles. For Queen and Country, we shall fall in line, tighten our belts, and keep our chins up.

With nigh twenty tonnes of cargo, we are not travelling light. We are: three white men, one white woman, one Wambutti guide, twenty-four askari soldiers, and roughly one hundred sixty carriers. I expect our numbers will convey strength, a party prepared to repel assault from man or beast.

We are additionally armed with plenty of trading stock—brass wire, cowrie shells, beads, and bolts of cloth for presents to help us pass unmolested. Also in store: swords, daggers, one Morris chair, 16-shooter American Winchesters and Remingtons with over 300 rounds per rifle, a breechloader elephant gun, iron trunks, axes, drag ropes, and photographic apparatus. In our possession, too, is a cedar water craft which breaks down into carry-able pieces; when assembled, it measures fifty-foot long with a seven-foot beam.

The Bambesi narrows daily. Without end we pass giant reeds and thick, vine-wrapped trees. Hornbills croak through the air, and here and there jut rocky outcrops that endanger our present vessel's hull. I cannot help but wonder if we have missed our turn, this being a generally uncharted region. Do you know Swift's rhyme?

*So geographers in Afric maps*
*With savage pictures fill their gaps,*
*And o'er inhabitable downs*
*Place elephants for want of towns.*

I never was much for even navigating London's bustling streets, map or no, but now that we have commenced we shall continue as best we can.

My Wambutti guide, Virgil, makes offerings to the river spirits and local devils. The chains of superstition hang heavy.

Some of the butterflies here are wonderful. In a manly sort of way, of course.

I have taken to short trousers. What is the proper length hereabouts? Just below the knee? Clue me in, if you would, Jepson. Along with their turbans, our Zanzibari carriers bustle about in caftans or skirts, but I do not think the look would work for me.

As a man unaccustomed to wielding authority—except in shushing an obstreperous library patron or two—at times I find myself at odds with my men. Captain Fuggleby, in particular, seems to regard me as someone who has killed his mum.

Therefore, I practice ordering Virgil about daily. He finds it great fun.

"Double-march!" I said recently. "We must make haste!"

He scampered to and fro about the creaking, weathered deck. Then he broke into laughter.

After a puff on my pipe, I could not help but smile myself.

"Indeed. Well done."

"Whoo!"

It was on my tongue to advise him to show some reserve. Instead, I joined in further.

"Huzzah! Splendid."

Frivolity aside, sir, let me assure you there is no truth to the rumour that the Government is ready to abandon your province. We do come. I suspect you do not hear much in the way of news. I know I miss my morning paper already. What is a pipe without a paper, I ask you?

I bring you a valise full of books, including Dr. Livingstone's volume, which I have been perusing. He mentions a twelve-year-old lad being sold in exchange for a single fowl.

Heavens, the perversity of human nature invites our compassion, does it not?

"Never say die," I tell my men. "There's no funeral without a corpse, and there's marvellous power in goodness."

I must close—Henry, a former tent-boy of Thorpe's, grows impatient for this despatch. I can only hope you and your men have not been enslaved, or anything similarly disagreeable.

Yours obediently,<br>H. R. Huxtable

P.S. Have you any recipes substituting local fowl into a dish bearing a semblance to pigeon pie? I am prepared for any upcoming danger, but I will not eat grubs or the like.

# LETTER IV.

*(Naro Moru Marsh Encampment, 29 April 1888;
received in London at the end of June, 1888)*

Dearest Florence—

Despite the oppressive sun here at the World's End, pumpkin,
I wear your woollen scarf yet.

Kina bomba (Greetings)! It has been a hectic day, my dearest.
I write you by oil lamp, resting within the confines of my humble
tent. I think of you nightly, laughing and arm-wrestling with
your fellow dockworkers—but rest assured, I think of you in the
day, too. How are you? You call yourself a "mannish woman,"
yet I care not. And as never before, I long to stroke your beefy
biceps. Your brawny limbs. Your... Well, all of you.

How is the vegetable-rights movement coming along? You
would thrill at the unmolested state of the wild fruits around
here.

We are at the World's End, and I am about at wit's end, too.

Tonight we bivouac near an extensive marsh and my walking-shoes are presently sopped. There are traces of the purity which reigned before the fall in this setting. On the other hand, it is a reeking Slough of Despond, with little in the way of shade. The gnats, flies, and other flying things are relentless. A number of these insects are almost big enough to hold one down.

As we encamped earlier, the sun burned in a cloudless sky, and the mud stink rose all around. Captain Muffin smashed a swarm of mosquitoes on his stout neck.

"Times like this I wonder why I ever came here," he said.

When first we met, he had purported to be a veteran of the Seventh Fusiliers. Yesterday, he claimed he hailed from the Eighth.

Now, I said, "To escape the authorities?"

He laughed darkly. The sweat stood in beads on his face.

"Hate this bloody swamp."

I commenced with my own frenzy of swatting.

"Success won't be handed to us on a velvet pillow, Captain. We must pay a price. Yet think of the glory that awaits!"

Except for the buzzing insects, there was a gaping silence. He threw me a grim look, a cleft between his brows.

Scratching at a welt on his wrist, he muttered, "Barmiest choice ever, encamping here."

For a moment I was tempted to swat at him.

"Don't be a rock round my neck," I said.

"Oh, I'm happy, happy, happy."

Given the conditions, Florence, I have supped on bananas—sorry, love—and dried fish and taken refuge under my solar topee (sun helmet) draped with netting. Rumours of a great Ape-Man abound in these regions. This very much excites our Miss Eaton.

"Good 'eavens!" she cries.

I spent this afternoon bird-watching. To date, I have noted the spotted cuckoo, the yellow wagtail, the blue drongo shrike, and—brace yourself—the brown kite and his piercing whistle! Ankle-deep in stagnant water, a sedgy aroma in the air, I delighted in the dancing flamingos—at least until I spied the glittering eyes and ridged back of a crocodile lurking in the mud. Still, given time, I should like to paint the scene with my watercolours.

This expeditioning is hard work. But I must admit the exertion enhances the charms of repose, mosquitoes or no.

Due to a narrowed channel, we were forced finally to abandon our rolling, creaking tub, the *Charity*. I was not sorry to part with our pilot, Hendricke. Yet the man did make off with our Union Jack.

Reunited now with the land party, we shall cut a road and find another waterway east, then break out our portable cedar craft. We—or the porters, in fact—were half the day unloading our assorted boxes, bales, and bundles. While supervising, each time I fell into a muck-hole, wallowing about, they laughed and snapped their fingers in merriment.

Never a master of mathematics, I have made a miscalculation or two. We have more general cargo than these men can possibly bear. Seeing that they are lazy and reluctant to carry loads over fifty pounds each, we may be forced to make double or triple journeys by short stages, until more help can be recruited.

These porters also smoke endless amounts of sweet-smelling cannabis. They roll it up in dun-coloured leaves. Along with the infernal heat, this herb use likely also slows us. In addition, to them time appears to have little measure, no reference points. Some goods may sink into the muck tonight.

This eve we light large fires to discourage the lions and hyenas. Our camp is a motley assortment of flickering shadows, boxes, tents, camp-stools, large tins, braying donkeys, and goats. Everything smells of wood smoke. I have word to be wary of carriers sneaking off with their loads during the evening, so I have posted night sentries, just in case.

Today I tried to obtain my first latitude reading by astronomical observations and triangulation—without much success. I had us in a line with Kowloon. Lofty twin peaks tipped with snow loom to our northeast. Before they disappeared in mist, Captain Muffin estimated their distance by prismatic compass-bearing to be twenty-five miles away.

He and my other high-spirited captain, one Fuggleby, are forever drinking and throwing fists at one another. Both are shabby and unshaven, with long, wild hair. They show no impatience to be moving, or general promptitude for labour. And they are forever testing and questioning my orders.

"We're on the same side, no?" I finally said to them, some days ago.

They stared back at me and shrugged.

"There's a war to win!" I said.

"War?" Muffin said, one eyebrow arched.

"Well, so to speak. And you will not—I repeat, will not—show me up in front of the others."

Their only response was to smack their lips as if they had thirst.

I do not know if they dislike taking orders from civilians of all stripe, or if it is the particulars of my private funding that engenders their resentment. Still, they save most of their ill temper for each other, and sometimes when they become engaged in abusing each other verbally and physically, a chuckle escapes me.

"Oh ho!" I say.

Truly, it takes two fools to argue. Their readiness to go to war at a moment's notice may prove a good thing.

Or it may prove a problem.

What I had not expected from them was such inflexibility. If I beckon our party to an early halt, Fuggleby calls it "the silliest damn rot" and the like. Or Muffin bursts out laughing and calls our mission "the biggest joke on record."

They do love their complaining. Last night as I passed Fuggleby's tent, I overheard them deriding me directly. The tent sat in a greenish gloom alongside a bamboo thicket. Unable to resist eavesdropping, I crouched by a tent wall. Though I could not see them, I imagined that, as usual, they looked haggard and ill.

"He's flipping useless," Fuggleby said on the other side of the canvas. "Ain't worth a fart in a whirlwind."

"He don't give a booger," Muffin said.

"He don't give a ding."

The rascals! Of course I give a ding. A few yards distant, a carrier squinted at me with suspicion, but I waved him away. Bitter smudge-pot smoke wafted out from between the tent flaps.

"Pass on that bottle!" Muffin said a moment later. "Wouldn't mind more of that. Aye, it's brain damage, rotgut, tastes like a sick man pissed in it—but it's the right stuff. Let's get drunk to the roof beams. Where was we?" He paused. "Oh! He don't give a monkey's."

I could not listen further to their sparkling conversation.

Yet when I turned, I bumped into a tent guide-rope.

"What was that?" Fuggleby said inside the tent.

I froze.

"You're hearing things," Muffin said. "Now, give me that bottle back again, or I'll knock you on your arse."

"Ah, I couldn't give a bucket of cow shit what you want."

"Well, why don't you go to hell and stay there?"

I waited for the inevitable. One, two...

A loud smack followed, and I departed under cover of the ensuing fisticuffs.

For now, I ignore their carping. Of course I am worth a fart in a whirlwind.

At day's end, they also slouch about the campfire with half-mast eyes, carousing with the porters. Perhaps they drink so much out of boredom; I too have found myself taking a few medicinal nips lately.

Despite his unruly vertical hair, Captain Muffin may be more civilised than Fuggleby. With his big jaws, he reminds me of a bulldog. Fuggleby seems to have a sneer ironed into his face.

Unlike them, the Zanzibaris are a handsome group, dear. Of lofty forehead, decked out in their odd-looking metal ornaments, they are striking.

In their devilish Kiswahili grammar, apparently they talk of Morungo, the Great Spirit who formed all things. Yet they chuckle when I kneel and pray aloud for guidance, asking who it is I talk to. Even when their eyes burn red from their cannabis smoking, there is a dignity to them. Therein lies the rub. They are resistant to too much bossing.

"We shall have peace through strength," I said to my ruddy-faced captains days ago, regarding avoiding any problems from these porters.

Fuggleby had trouble looking me in the eye. Although he grinned, his expression did not signify agreement.

"Of course, sir."

Muffin clapped his heels lazily together and saluted, then erupted in laughter. With his own mock deference, Fuggleby pulled off his sun helmet and bowed.

"Heavens, make yourselves useful and get the men organised," I said. "Smart discipline will get us—"

"These men?" Fuggleby scowled. "Ain't never seen a bigger crowd of laggards. Fine specimens, indeed!"

He, I should add, is one of the biggest dawdlers himself.

I waved the fools off.

Though more dignified than my captains (not the most Herculean achievement), there is a prankish side to the Zanzibaris. Today they coaxed me into setting my cot up over a nest of red ants. Before long, sparks of fire in my trousers rudely interrupted my nap. I jumped about, tearing off my clothes like a prime candidate for Bedlam, to the evident enjoyment of everyone save myself.

With his fiddle, Virgil often joins the Zanzibaris around the fire. Together they sing songs about their bedroom feats. Is it the heat which brings out all this idle sexual chatter?

Which brings me to Miss Eaton, purportedly of the Christians for Celibacy Society. Ha! The woman is half barmy, if not fully so, and seems more interested in celebrating savage customs than suppressing them.

She has taken to wearing outrageous amounts of glass beads and copper bracelets. Even here in the wilderness, she wears more cosmetic paint than the few female savages we have glimpsed. When I asked her if she had given Bibles to the Zanzibaris, she laughed as if I had made a great joke.

Speak of the devil, she peeks through my tent flap now, Florence.

"Some people 'as it easy," she screeches as I shoo her away. "When I saw you sitting there, I thought you was working!"

Her brown curls sprouting out from under her helmet like Medusa's snaky locks, she leers at all of us, a regular fag artist puffing away on one Ogden's Guinea Gold cigarette after another. The Methodist Anti-Cigarette League would be appalled at her consumption. And somehow she knows not that impure urges are reserved for men.

I do fancy her long brown leather boots. The day she insisted on bathing naked before us and asked me to fetch them, something about them stimulated me, and I have thought of them often since.

I do not mean to incur your jealousy with these stories, precious. And I suppose I should not make sport of her.

Virgil, my guide, interpreter, and general aide-de-camp, remains indispensable. Game-bird tied to his belt with a vine, he grins and promises me hippo meat soon. Not long ago he served up a roasted monkey. Needless to say, I refrained from spooning any brain. I have provided him with Mrs. Godfrey's *Book of Household Management*, and he and the cooks have managed some fine puddings and the like.

It has begun to occur to me that not speaking any of the native dialects myself may prove a problem. For instance, Virgil recently informed me that the porters have dubbed me "Big-Nosed White Man." Until then I had thought I cut rather a dashing figure in my helmet, short trousers, and puttees.

A short while ago Virgil joined me for afternoon tea outside my tent, and served up a tale of hands and feet in a cooking pot.

"We must take care," he said, after regaling me with a number of unsavoury details. "This is Land of Look-Behind. And tribes here are fearing us as evil."

We sipped in silence. In the distance moved big purple and pink clouds. After a day of trudging through thorny thickets and hurtful grass, I was knackered and wanted never to arise from my camp-chair.

We would slash a route on the morrow, plunging further into a land marked "Unknown" on the map. Divine benevolence and monsters of the forest permitting, we would succeed, I assured him as we savoured our tea.

"We will save this Jepson," he said, his eyes shining. "We will, Mr. Huxtable!"

I looked at him sideways, considering, as he dunked a lump of hard bread into his cup. I packed and lit my pipe, then rubbed my chin manfully. Along with my hickory tobacco, I could smell the muck of the nearby marsh, blended with the sour odour of old sweat which we both exuded.

"You don't understand, don't see the rest of it, do you?" I said. "We also do this for the Queen."

"Oh?"

"And Country."

He twisted his mouth to one side.

"Hmm. To me, to save this man Jepson is something good enough."

"Indeed. Well, I suppose proving worthy's all I want."

"Our time will come, I know it."

I puffed on my pipe, my eyes never leaving his face, then said, "Something else is on your mind."

"Your captains?"

I flicked away a buzzing fly.

"Yes?"

Wearing a serious expression, he shook his head and let out a low whistle. He carried a pouch of herbs on his belt, which he screwed between his fingers.

"Watch them—I think they are *murenga*."

"What? Are what?"

"How do you say?" he said, an undercurrent of concern in his lowered voice. "They…resist. Their presence maybe we need fear. Also I hear Captain Muffin argue."

"So? He and Fuggleby are always at each other."

"When all alone."

I thought about this, then said firmly and with great authority, "They are men of shallow understanding. Perhaps *they* need to fear Hubert Reginald Huxtable."

Until I return, dear, for want of the real man, you may hold this scrappy letter to your bosom. (You may put it down, too, of course; we shall be adventuring a while.)

Your Gallant Librarian,

Hubert

# LETTER V.

*(From H. R. Huxtable to the Staff of the Royal Order of the Muskrat Memorial Library, undated)*

Dear colleagues, friends, fellow bookworms—

Greetings! How is life on the damp isle, and how are our snoozing patrons? I sometimes miss the splendid boredom— the bow-tied and tailcoated gentlemen sunk in their easy chairs, rarely rousing themselves enough to read anything more than the daily news, and so on. Have any been discovered deceased lately? I must admit always having been reluctant to disturb those found newly dead; I wished we could just tuck them away under a "Quiet!" sign somewhere, books propped on their laps, to read in peace through all eternity.

I shall never forget the time Squire Goodman sat dead to the world, not ten feet away from my reference desk, without me noticing for several hours that he had checked out on us. I was never much for Bulwer-Lytton's writing either, but it never induced anything near a fatality in me.

To be frank, before I accepted this present adventure, I truly feared losing my esteemed library position. For the record, I still vehemently deny absconding with that volume of bawdy etchings. What rubbish! (I did spend some time examining it—quite some time, perhaps—but never did I remove it from the premises.) Without other prospects, I feared ending up one of those sandwich-board men, carrying advertisements about in the streets for a few shillings a day.

But here in the wilds of Africa, I am "Nyamatimbira": I am a master. At the present moment, though, I shake like a starved and poorly kept servant. This is due to almost dying this afternoon myself, in a heart-stopping encounter with a charging rhino.

The whole affair greatly tested my nerves.

The lurid details, as it were, are as follows.

In order to maintain a veneer of civility, I had insisted on a midday tea break from our march. A lovely earthy smell perfumed the air after a brief deluge. Insects clicked and chirped. I reclined in my Morris chair, perusing a tome on birdsong and drying my soggy feet over a kindling fire. (The fire was an afterthought provided through the kindness—or so I naively first believed—of Captain Fuggleby.) At my side, my aide-de-camp, Virgil, squatted, playing upon the bamboo whistle which hangs from his necklace.

All of a sudden I heard a great tramp of feet and much shouting. And upon looking up from my book, I discovered through my cracked spectacles a puffing, snorting rhino rapidly closing the distance.

Bugger!

The beast thundered right for me. Driving up clods of earth, its hooves leaped off the ground. Inside its huge mouth loomed teeth bigger than railroad spikes.

Virgil later confessed he nearly swallowed his whistle. I am certain that, had my body not been frozen, I would have fouled my trousers.

My life—sedate till then—passed before my very eyes as the immense creature closed in.

This never would have happened if I had stayed in foggy London! Why had I not at least read up on these beasts within the library's cosy confines before coming? Virgil had warned me they could crush most anything, but that was the extent of my knowledge.

"With them," he had said, "it's over before it starts."

So, I prepared to meet my end.

Thanks be to God, a quick-thinking askari grabbed the loaded elephant rifle and discharged it.

Nonetheless, falling out of my beloved chair in fright was the only thing that saved me. The charging beast finally crashed to a dead halt at my reading spot, as if upon an intended target.

My Morris chair suffered greatly. In the process, the beast even smashed my watercolour set. And I never did get my feet dried.

I shall send you a photographic picture of the dead rhino and wounded chair, when processed. Perhaps you could post it on the library's "Miscellaneous Excitements" board.

"Mr. Huxtable, you all right?" Virgil said afterwards.

Was I all right? An enraged rhino had assaulted me! I would never be all right.

I could only blink at him.

"Fine," I finally managed to say.

Thank heavens for my Mrs. Winslow's Soothing Syrup! After the incident, I slugged down half of a bottle.

Later, Virgil informed me of the rhino's natural penchant to charge in and stamp upon any fires it comes across.

I must assume the scoundrel Fuggleby knew this full well, considering the effort he went to in starting me a fire, after first borrowing my field glasses—likely to verify the presence of rhinos about.

"It's too bloody hot for a fire," I had said.

"Nonsense, sir. Our leader must have dry feet!"

Indirectly, he has inspired me to come up with a unique idea that might be employed by the London Fire Brigade. But before long the man may, like my chair, need a straightening out.

Lately, I wonder whether he functions on the level of a lower nervous organisation, like reptiles. Or fungi.

As a matter of fact, we are camping here, on a plain opposite red cliffs—though this is not a colour I prefer—due to a spat between Fuggleby and Captain Muffin. Given the region's dangerous nature, Muffin recommends breaking our caravan into squads of twenty, while Fuggleby adamantly insists on squads of thirty. All of this is for the sake of argument, I take it.

The discrepancy in opinion led to a good fistfight, but no forward progress. Providence and Muffin, hand in hand, inflicted the desired punishment on Fuggleby, yet neither will budge on the issue. Muffin is pigheaded, certainly, but this Fug-gleby is a bloody bonehead.

"Heavens," I said, after calling them together to my tent. They both looked the worse for drink. Fuggleby's face also revealed a bounty of lumps. "Do you two always have to make such a damned fuss?"

As always, their immediate response was simple contradiction.

"Ain't so," Muffin said.

"A damned fuss," Fuggleby said. "A damned fuss? You're bloody daft!"

Two trained monkeys might have proved more useful.

"Captain Fuggleby, I will not abide gratuitous insults," I said. "If you want trouble, keep talking."

"Yes, sir."

"That counts as—"

"I suppose it does."

I threw him a narrow-eyed look of displeasure, but said no more.

We shall bivouac and sleep on—or sleep off—the issue.

"'I may hate meself in the morn," Muffin told me, gasping as he prepared to retire to his tent. "Perhaps I should sleep in till noon."

All unruly yellow locks and a face that appears forever bruised, the man is an original, if nothing else.

For now I will avoid further showdown with either captain. I will not give them the satisfaction, and I have the mission to think of. Still, I see further discord and danger ahead.

Besides my Morris chair, we have had two recent casualties. The first was a porter who succumbed to a well-disguised hippo trap. The man tripped off a large suspended beam armed with a spearhead.

As I eyed his impaled body, my shirt dampened with sweat. There, but for the grace of God, went I. Dressed in a pale blue robe and turban, now rather purple with blood, the man was dead as Squire Goodman at the library. I could not look him in the face. Bloody hell. I felt a sense of a dark force spreading its wings.

Beneath the high, hot sun, I swallowed and scanned the path ahead. To either side of us, steep canyon walls edged our route.

What other traps lay before us? Were we all to perish? Would any of us even reach Fort Bim?

Suddenly the sky turned grey, then black. The heavens opened up, and rain fell, hard.

"Just keep going!" I called out.

Thunder cracked across the sky. The rain drove into our faces, nigh blinding us.

We slogged on.

It began to pour harder, although that did not seem possible. Our muscles stiffened from the dampness. The mud sucked at our feet and legs. That night the howling winds blew down our tents, yet in our exhaustion we slept on.

The next day, a young man gone for water staggered back to camp with a hideous barbed spear in his side. He expired soon after, which was a definite inconvenience, as he had not returned with the needed water.

I have warned the men to be more careful.

Our trip up the Bambesi was not without incident, either: for days I suffered a horrible bowel complaint.

Besides my unruly, toad-witted captains and the local savages, I also have worries with the porters. They take to their load-bearing well, but my headman explains that they demand a load lightening. They note I refuse to carry anything more than my field glasses. And they say they do not understand where the term "the White Man's Burden" comes from, seeing as it is they who bear all.

I can feel their agitation. Although we pay them partly in cloth, they have referred to the fabric as "villainous." Poor quality, they mean, I gather.

At first, I had taken these porters to be tractable. Yet already they begin to whine like social reformers.

"Toleka, toleka!" I say. ("Let's go, let's go," in their tongue.) "Sound the horn! At the double! No room for grumblers or shirkers."

"Hurry, hurry, makes bad luck," they say.

"Remember the sufferings of Christ," I reply. "To save Governour Jepson, there're no mountains we won't climb, no deserts we won't cross. Or we'll die in the effort, as Providence may order."

To exhort my captains I occasionally call, "Pub ahead!"

Troubles aside, ours is a strange cavalcade—soldiers singing, carriers shouting, captains quibbling. Carrying our baggage overland and through the Naro Moru Marsh proved an ordeal. The porters' skirts packed with mud. The marsh birds stirred in panic. Insects assailed us without cease, and our fly-whisks had little effect on them. As Virgil led my donkey and me by the halter, he jested about leading two jackasses at once. (I would not tolerate such cheek from anyone else.)

Rioting vegetation, men, bales, donkeys, baggage—and the irrepressible Miss Eaton—it all makes quite a spectacle.

"So many sweaty men!" she has cried out more than once.

The Zanzibaris move gracefully, the whole line swaying like a long serpent.

Though she claims to enjoy riding, Miss Eaton occasionally dismounts from her peculiar custom-made saddle and squeezes a buttock or two.

Up front, an advance guard clears the way for our main body. With billhooks they slash at the brush. Trusty rifles in arm, others watch for cannibals. Often we can smell pungent elephant dung. We have no flag for a standard-bearer to carry, but Virgil promises me he is working on a new banner to replace our stolen Union Jack.

For your general information, our schedule is thus: camp, cook, sleep, strike camp, march. We travel a new route into unexplored land—the heart of sin and darkness. Due to the scuffle between my captains, today we halted on a small plain. The ground is baked hard. The grass is scorched. After the long day's ride, my buttocks are sore.

Visible through my field glasses is a drop to an open plateau, which overlooks what may be the north end of Lake Tikka. Under the sun the lake gleams like a golden mirror.

A look to our southeast (?) reveals the Valley of Wild Asses, and stony uplands beyond. There must be navigable rivers about here somewhere. But for the immediate desolate area, the region has revealed an exuberance of strange birds, beasts, flowers, and trees.

Sometimes I find it hard to believe the world was made in six days. I hope to find time to ponder this and also add to my burgeoning butterfly collection.

Today, thanks as I say to Muffin and Fuggleby, we have had more of a walk than a true march. We encountered one abandoned mud hut. Inside I could still smell the dead embers of a recent fire. Groundnuts dried in a woven basket. Though encumbered with copious baggage and provisions ourselves, we must not dawdle. We may have to coerce the porters to double-marches.

Success, however under Providence, depends on us as civilised Englishmen.

I do not add "and a civilised Englishwoman," mind you. I sometimes think our Miss Eaton not British but devil. Often naughty as a rude Brighton picture postcard, she proves a regular distraction. (I would advise you to skip this section, Miss Hoople, but suspect you will not.)

Recently, I could not help overhearing her and Virgil in the tent next to mine:

"Can't wait to 'ave it inside me," she cooed.

"It is inside, Miss Eaton."

"Oh, yes. Well, so it is."

I may be mistaken, but I do not think they were boning up on grammar. (Are you blushing yet, Miss Hoople? No? Read on, then.)

For reducing her freckles, Miss Eaton swears by Dr. Simm's Arsenic Complexion Wafers. At times I suspect their use has somehow accentuated her animal propensities.

To be fair, the woman has some culture. She talks of putting on a recital of Machiavelli's *Mandragola*. In fact, yesterday she and I began a rehearsal. As she joined me, her straw bonnet barely cleared my commodious tent's ceiling. The afternoon sun spread a warm yellow light through the rolled tent flaps.

Despite the steamy air, for the occasion I had smartened myself up and donned my plaid sack coat. I chose a Guyot brace to hold up my trousers.

"Wisely done!" she had me enunciate, pointing at the text in her hand.

Slyly, she sidled over to my fold-up writing table. Before I could object, she tucked my photographic image of Florence under my Bible, then returned to our recital.

"I made 'im undress," she said. "'e was whimpering. I turned on 'im like a dog so that it seemed a thousand years to 'im before 'e could strip off 'is clothes, and 'e stood there naked." She sucked lasciviously on her sticky lozenge, and in her excitement skipped a line or two. "You never saw such beautiful flesh! White, soft, smooth—and about the rest—don't ask me, mate!"

(It is said a lot of shouting and hullabaloo may keep a lion away. I imagine her general delivery would suffice, too. And, of course, I am quite certain Machiavelli never used the word "mate.")

After she gave me a sharp pinch, I read back to her.

"It's better not to talk about it. For everything has to be examined."

She gestured grandiloquently. She smashed a buzzing fly to a bloody mess and wiped her hand on her daisy-patterned skirt.

"You're pulling me leg!" she then emoted. "Since I 'ad stuck me 'and in the dough, I wanted to touch bottom. I wanted to be sure 'e was 'ealthy. Suppose 'e 'ad sores, where would I be? You tell me!"

"You're absolutely right!'" I read, but at the thought of those type of sores, I recoiled.

Did other great explorers ever end up in situations like this?

She touched my fingers for a moment. Her eyes were lit up.

"As soon as I 'ad made sure 'e was 'ealthy, I dragged 'im after me and led 'im to the bedroom in the dark…"

At this point, she appeared moved by our recital. Quite moved. Our heads were close together, and she glanced up briefly into my eyes. Her cheeks flushed. The tops of her bosoms were displayed like cakes on a platter.

From within her full mouth came more excited lozenge-sucking.

Was she about to undo the small black buttons of her bodice? Did she plan to fully reveal her Cupid's kettle drums?

I began to suspect the woman wanted my intrepid body.

Her probing hand further tipped me off.

Somehow until now I had missed the prettiness of her wide mouth, the pleasing delicacy of her nose. As her hand settled on its intended target, I gazed into her bold grey eyes for what may have been an improper amount of time.

I gave a little gasp of pleasure, yet managed at last to say, "Propriety, Miss Eaton. Propriety!"

"Oh, Mr. Huxtable!"

"Miss—"

Our lips met.

Heavens!

Had I eaten today any of the foods well known to excite the animal passions? Rich gravy? No. Pepper? No. Mustard?

Mustard! Drat!

Her skin smelled of a sweet dusting powder. Her grasping hand felt marvellous. And those bosoms…

As we broke for air, I said "Miss Eaton! We must set a—"

"Hush."

With another kiss, her wet, lemony lozenge found its way into my own stimulated mouth.

Soon, though, I came to my senses. I did resist. And I ushered her unceremoniously from my tent.

Yet alone later, I had impure thoughts. Those silky curls, those fetching curves! Her warm, grasping hand!

I nearly engaged in solitary vice.

Instead, I splashed water on my face and reminded myself of the dignity required of an emissary of the Royal Order of the Muskrats, and the importance of our mission. I must dedicate my body, mind, and will solely to its success.

This may require abandoning the entire dramatic project.

Just this morning, while being pursued by our determined female and her snaky curls, to ford a channel I was forced to escape by skipping from the back of one lazing crocodile to another—a feat applauded briefly but enthusiastically by the men.

Even in a voluminous skirt, she was both nimble and speedy.

"How very ridiculous you are!" I shouted over my shoulder as I departed. "I must decline your salacious offer and bid you good day."

"Come back, dear heart!" she cried.

With a protruding-toothed smile, Virgil tells me she awaits "pleasant intercourse with the tribes." (There is the word, Miss Hoople. Are you happy now?) Miss Eaton insists women should have a voice, and rights. Other women may bow and scrape—but not her. And I cannot deny she may be onto something there.

Well, I must toodle-oo for now.

(First, though, I would like to enclose a final message solely for Miss Hoople: Ma'am, I always felt you were working against me. Alas, this proved specially true the day we battled over the proper arrangement of the Round Reading Room's tables. Yes, I struck you with that fine volume of Thackeray. Yet you truly left me no recourse.)

As I wrap up this letter, I detect a piney smell that means rain is coming again. Nonetheless, as always, we must march on the morrow.

Say hello to our fusty patrons for me. Dust them regularly.

Yours sincerely,<br>Hubert H.

# LETTER VI.

*(From Governour G. Jepson to H. R. Huxtable, dated 3 May 1888, and delivered via runner and trained turkey vulture)*

Huxtable–

What is this letter of yours about, you blockheaded ninny? You sound like a prude in need of a good thrashing. Contrary to your assertions, we at Fort Bim are not like rats in a trap at all. For the most part we lead a free and happy life, enjoying certain indigenous luxuries even. The soldiers are married and flabby; several have harems. So we are unwilling to come away. Where did you come by the idea that we are in need of saving? Did you grow up in a sinister orphanage?

As to your other unfounded insinuations, I assure you there are no corrupt officers to be found here, and there has been no rebellion; the sun must be getting to you. If this is to be some kind of war of wits, I would venture you are in trouble. Of course the Government is not ready to abandon the province. We have a quarter battalion of regulars dispersed throughout the region, manning the fort and three stations, and they are all good men. We are, you might say, entrenched.

What is this talk of the Mahdi and your concocted stories about the Arab threat? Since Gordon's fall, he and Khartoum together, there has been some devastation on our outskirts—but none affecting us directly. A few weeks hence, the Mahdi's people, in the form of three whirling dervishes, did make an attempt on my life, but they were quickly fitted with irons.

If you continue, you will be the one who winds up on the Ibo slave market. Your proposed route is laughable. The jungle is for real men, Huxtable.

If you do manage to live long enough to reach us, which I think highly unlikely, I will see you flogged for stupidity. I take you for a man of Science, Commerce, and Philanthropy, which virtually guarantees you have no survival skills. I suppose you think you open the way for the gospel, too. What rubbish.

There are cannibals in your path, you know. (Fee-fi-fo-fum, they can smell the blood of Englishmen.) Lunatics like you from the Continent remind me why I first left. You are not worthy of the attentions of my parrot.

May your boat sink in crocodile-infested waters. You shall certainly starve, at the very least.

Most sincerely,

G. Jepson

# LETTER VII.

*(From H. R. Huxtable to the Chairman
of the Jepson Relief Committee, undated,
received in London, June 1888)*

My Dear Murchison—

How are you, sir? I have had a concerning communication from
Jepson. (I believe it is from him, but I will get to that shortly.)
We may have a problem—the man said he hoped my boat sank
in crocodile-infested waters. Yet for my good nature, I should
like to clobber him with the valise of books that I intended to
gift him with. He also relates there is no Arab Mahdi threat.

Still, the letter may be a forgery. Or he may have been forced
by captors to write in this impertinent manner to ward off our
party. The Mahdists may kill him yet.

If this missive is not a deception, the man is clearly not a soul
awake to influences higher than Earth. And it may be that he
is engaged in illicit activity.

Either way, I wanted the Relief Committee to know our force may not be met with a smile and open arms. There may have been a mix-up somewhere. Yet we shall proceed onward nonetheless.

Shortly after reading the abominable letter, at a halt in our march I sought out my trusty guide, Virgil. Red dust mixed with sweat ran in muddy streaks down his face as he unwrapped a small rectangular leaf packet, and we dug our fingers into the rank-smelling but life-sustaining cassava paste inside it.

"We'll get to the bottom of this," I said, as we licked the starchy mush from our fingers.

He frowned. As always, the sounds of the jungle surrounded us: thumps, crashes, and animal calls came from the trees, and insects chittered from every direction. A spatter of rain began to fall, smacking the big leaves of the trees.

"Of course."

"Can't let anything disrupt us." I wiped my mouth with one of my few remaining handkerchiefs. "And what about our soldiers? Do they connive in dark corners?"

"No."

I breathed out a sigh of relief. The gruelling strain of the march, coupled with the heat, had eaten away at most everyone's outlooks. Lately I could scarcely keep track of the rumours and counter-rumours. Even the clouds have conspired lately, assaulting us with violent winds. At least the askari soldiers—ever ready with their ammunition belts and rifles—were behind me.

"Jolly good."

Fingering his necklace, Virgil gave a grunt.

"They talk in open now."

A nasty feeling of tightness came upon my skin.

"Heavens, here's a state of affairs. Well, let them talk till their tongues drop out." I let out a little laugh—nerves, maybe. "Perhaps we all need to smoke the cannabis?"

Since I last wrote, life has grown stranger. When we are at riverside, bloated dead native bodies float past us—likely the ghastly handiwork of Arab slavers. There are ghost villages and mighty coils of evil about.

A few days prior, we came upon a sole survivor of one of these raids. Young, yet with a distant look in his eyes, the man refused our help. Not far away lay a broken Arab brandy bottle.

We left him with a Bible.

Afterwards, we traversed a long stretch of grassland and hill country. Since neither of my tetchy captains would compromise on marching in squads of twenty-five daily, on odd days we travelled in squads of twenty, on even days in squads of thirty.

At times, though, they argued over which day it was.

So after we encamped one day, I called them to my tent.

The past series of hours had proved hard going, and I had just settled a tobacco-distribution dispute. We would never succeed if I did not keep our party close-knit and disciplined, so it was up to me to exert control.

The situation with these two louts had to change. I could not make the mistake of trusting them—if they ever sobered up, who knew what infernal machinations they might engage in against me? Perhaps it is a good thing they can barely agree on the colour of the sky.

Yet if I reprimanded them too harshly now, would our noble expedition grind to a halt?

"Cease your fighting, Captains. I cannot abide it, will not abide it." I mopped my brow. Not far away turbaned Zanzibaris tended to cook-fires before a swath of dense forest. "And that is an order. We must bash on."

They both (surprise, surprise!) found the ground beneath their feet a little unstable, and they gave off the stink of gin as they stared blankly at me with glazed eyes. Dried sweat caked their ruddy faces, which were half-hidden in their matted beards. Their khaki tunics were soiled and torn.

After a brief moment Fuggleby made a sound—it seemed to signal discontent—but voiced no outright opposition.

"That understood?" I said.

After some eye-rolling, they muttered what might have been affirmations. Smoke drifted over from the open cook-fires as I placed my hands together, fingertips to fingertips.

"May I add another word?"

"Oh, please," Fuggleby slurred.

I spoke now with exaggerated patience, as if explaining to not-very-bright children.

"I don't wish to make an uncivil reflexion on your efforts thus far, but I must say they've been…lacking. I value you both. Still, you do not exactly bristle with efficiency."

Muffin snorted.

"Value this," Fuggleby said, and released gas from his posterior.

As Muffin responded with a loud laugh, I sighed deeply and abstained from a strong desire to cover my eyes with my hand. A commander has to maintain a certain dignity, and I did not want to appear overly delicate.

"Captains! My orders are to be obeyed. I need my officers to be audacious! Aggressive on the march! We can't afford to sit around twiddling our thumbs. We must move like the wind, must quickstep like the hare!"

"Oh my," Fuggleby said. "You going to blather on now about 'For the Queen!' and all that airy nonsense?"

"Enough! On the morrow we commence again. You're meant to be leaders. Herein, men, let's work together. We must not have fear of work, hard work." They remained silent and I gathered I was impressing them at last. "Indeed, it may not be bloody easy—but there's the challenge, there it is."

Muffin rubbed his belly and belched.

"And jeopardise not the coin you're here for," I said. "Now, anyone for cocoa and biscuits?"

"I think not," Muffin said.

Fuggleby lifted his dark brows with disbelief. Without any warning he fell down. In a moment he dragged himself up again.

With a wave of my hand, I dismissed them. They stumbled moodily towards their own tents.

"Cocoa!" I heard Fuggleby say in the distance. He uttered a scornful burst of laughter. "Oh my, there'll come a time."

(Afterwards followed profanities from him I will not record.)

Meanwhile, I have tried to obtain further latitude readings, again without much success. We have had confusion as to our course. There is a slight possibility I have been holding my map upside-down for the past several days, yet I know the Valley of Wild Asses is about here somewhere.

I do not like maps.

It happens I am not much for tumultuous rivers either—one noisy cataract after another, whirlpools, eddies.

After painstakingly assembling our watercraft, which I had dubbed the *Lady Florence*, it came time to test my naval skills on the Iluri River. As we launched our oar-equipped vessel, the day was dry, the view clear.

At first the river, about eighty yards wide, glided over pale gravel. Mild rapids separated flat stretches. Rags of grey cloud drifted through the jungle-clad hills, and a heron soared downstream ahead of us.

Smooth passage, fully in command—it all felt sublime.

Yet soon we rounded a bend, and the river narrowed. The waters thundered.

As we dropped into a chaos of roaring white, I turned first green (I suspect), then queasy. Grey rocks hurtled past. Water crashed round our vessel.

Wildly, at the tiller I steered this way and that. The men pulled at their oars for all they were worth.

"Row hard!" I said as the ripping and snorting current whipped us around a bend.

There were the lives of many in my hands. Yet an ice-cold animal fear consumed me.

Our boat dipped into the waves. Then it buoyed back up. Hardly breathing, I could feel us accelerating madly, sliding downhill. We bumped, we bounced. It was as if mighty fists pounded at our hull.

Swells rolled towards us and broke over the sides.

Promptly, the *Lady Florence* grounded upon an unfriendly boulder.

"Dash my wig!" I exclaimed.

This was keenly disappointing. Suddenly I did not want to go one foot further with this quest. I yearned for the cobblestone streets of London; I longed for the safe confines of the Memorial Library.

But I knew I had to go on: we had a moral task to fulfil, and there could be no turning back.

In my mind I heard a gate clang shut behind us. Retreat was no option.

Fortunately, we wrecked close to shore. We shuttled off most of the cargo before the boat fully smashed up. Alas, it splintered on the rocks and was sucked into a whirlpool. Waves covered it. Not a word was uttered by anyone as we gazed at the spot where it went down. I am afraid the men were unimpressed with this, my first piloting experience.

I wished there were safer ferries about.

For want of that, we commandeered a number of long canoes found hidden in a plantain grove. During this seizure, we were assailed by a confusion of stones, launched by pesky native children.

Afterwards, I was not surprised when my men crossed their dusky arms to their chests and said: "We do not want to shoot down the fast water like an arrow again."

Above us the sky was a dazzling, bright blue. The image of the *Lady Florence* dashing to pieces, so much whirlpool-fodder, lay fresh on my brain.

"A capital notion." I nodded my head, showing a most decided agreement. "Only too glad to oblige your request, men. As for my piloting? I regret we did not fare as well as I expected."

These new dugouts enable us to paddle from one set of rapids to another, then portage around them.

We were near the Po-po rapids and falls, Virgil told me. We had to be careful. Surly tribes resided on each bank.

Near noon today, he and I watched from the riverside as two mud-daubed men speared a hippo from their craft. As we spied through the reeds, the assaulted hippo bellowed in agony. The scene reminded me again of my troubled Aunt Edna back home—all the beast lacked was an embroidered handkerchief to blow its nose into.

Skulking there, I also thought back to the queer letter I had received from Jepson. Did something horrible await us ahead, too?

With the danger, we are all flaring tempers lately. I have overheard some of my actions being discussed by the few English-speaking Zanzibaris, and it was not at all to my advantage. I find it difficult not to drop barbed remarks myself.

Of course, my captains were temperamental to begin with. Perhaps it is best that they march at our column's front, rifles in hand, while I command from the rear.

Yet I will not shrink from demanding compliance. We can only survive through discipline.

Save for an occasional spearing or mutilation, our days are filled with a creeping sameness. Due to the daytime heat, our cook-fires are lit in 4:00 a.m. darkness. We march or paddle a few miles early in the morn, rest from the sun, and quarrel in the afternoon.

One recent midday, Muffin met me with a specially surly greeting, followed by words of outright abuse. I could overlook some insolence—but only so much.

I clenched the edge of the map I had been examining from various angles and shook my head. Contempt showed in his rheumy eyes.

It was clear he needed to be taken down a peg.

"You're courting trouble with your foolishness, Captain," I said. "Must I remind you? This mission is a—"

"Taking orders from a bloody…librarian?"

When he spat the last word out as the worst form of insult, I felt blood rushing to my head.

The jowly fool! I doubted the man could withstand the rigours of relentless cataloguing and book restoration.

"You—and everyone else—will follow my—"

"A librarian! Makes me want to spew."

"Betray our mission, sir, and you betray yourself. My orders will be obeyed."

He stood silent, but with his lips pressed tightly together. One of his eyes twitched.

Lately, the man appears stressed beyond reason. I will keep a sharp eye on him. Virgil, with his pouches of ground bark and seeds to ward off evil, addresses the captain in a kind way. He advises him to carry cassava seeds to keep away the spirits that bring madness. Yet Muffin will hear none of it.

Later that afternoon, I heard his strained voice in the distance.

"You shabby devil!"

From within the dark forest façade, Fuggleby responded.

"You're a blooming liar!"

"I tell you, Fuggleby, you're a bloody bastard. Don't go sticking your ugly mug where you ain't wanted. Or I'll beat you like a drum."

After their most recent row, Fuggleby was already missing the tip of one ear; Muffin's nose now canted to one side. I wondered if I should have them strip to the waist and hold daily bare-knuckle boxing matches, and thus entertain our entire force while they exercised their ill humours.

Instead, I moved closer and through the bush called them both to order, not without asperity.

And to improve spirits and reduce ructions, the following late morn I called our entire force together at a grassy clearing along the Haroni River. With flawless blue sky overhead, for a dramatic touch, I ascended a sizeable grey boulder.

From one day to the next, I never knew just where the unrest would bloom, so it was vital to impress my authority and determination on the entire company. Vital!

Below and all around me, white, violet, and mauve fezzes and turbans dotted the clearing. Only a few feet away from my sun-warmed boulder, tiny yellow flowers adorned Miss Eaton's sun helmet. I could smell the hickory tobacco Virgil and I often shared, but I did not see him. My trusty captains, I imagined, were slugging down gin within the tree line.

"All I have, all I am, is the ground I stand on," I said in a loud, clear voice. "Or should I say the boulder I stand on? Indeed. Hmm." Flies settled on my sweaty face and I brushed them off. I thumped one hand into the other. "Well! Anyway, we'll not give ground—and we'll push forward against any opposition."

For plentiful minutes, I treated them with my oration. Hubert Reginald Huxtable had them enthralled! Of course at other times they grew surly due to their workloads—but doubtless now they could not help but look up at me with utmost awe. Clouds of cannabis smoke drifting by, I posed with both hands aloft. In my excitement, I may have even waggled my bum. (Hopefully I did not show any of that stimulation in my nether regions.)

The air trembled, undulated. The sun climbed higher.

Beneath my feet the boulder began to radiate heat like an oven. To gain some relief, I lifted one foot then the other.

The entire crowd listened with rapt concentration. Even the big-beaked marabou storks in the nearest trees appeared impressed. Oh, how I expostulated! Some of the men knowing English may have cheered in approval. Some likely clapped. On my elevated perch—waving my arms about, hair pasted down on my head, blotched with sweat, marching in place—I was so full of words it seems I did not discern.

Nor did I maintain a steady footing.

About to issue a hearty huzzah, I fell. And I hit the ground with a thud.

The crowd cheered—thoroughly impressed by my oration, I gathered.

Flat on my back, for a moment I was uncertain if I had broken the entirety of my skeleton. Nothing hurt—or perhaps it was that everything hurt at once so I could differentiate no particular pain.

I lay there in the grass. I blinked my eyes. Each intake of my breath was half a groan.

My ears buzzed.

Above me, Miss Eaton stared down with a concerned look. After some time I managed to speak.

"Everyone—that is all!"

"Oh, dear," she said. "You all right?"

"Think I shall...lie here a while."

There was a silence between us.

Along with distant voices, I heard the murmur of the swift river.

"Quite the speech," she said at last.

Despite the abrupt, painful ending, I hoped my oration would help keep us together. For if we fight each other, what chances do we have of repelling the natives?

The hidden natives in mind, the days that followed were sombre—thickly misted, with everything still as death and silent as a grave. One almost seemed to hear one's heartbeat aloud.

"We must stay calm," I reminded all. "Fortune favours the brave."

Immersed in a cauldron of heat, my men constantly muttering, the *Lady Florence* down, potato-sized blisters on my feet, and sore all over from my tumble—it seemed things could not get any worse.

I was wrong.

Decked out in their bandoliers, the askaris appeared itchy for a fight with the natives. When we rested, they fussed over their rifles; one also heard the whining scrape of knife blades being whetted on stones. I was in no hurry to engage the locals myself, though Virgil promised to be my gun bearer. He readied himself with fresh poison for his darts (dried red ants, ground and cooked in palm oil, he related).

"They come soon," he told me. "I don't know when, but they come soon."

I nodded, my heartbeat increasing.

This expeditioning is a game of nerves.

If only we had our magnets! Before our departure, the Earl of Leicester had promised us that the science of magnetism could be used to put to sleep any savages we encountered. Alas, the same week he died, face down in his soup. Perhaps he was a victim of his own clever experiments?

At my instruction, Virgil left twisted wisps of grass about. This is a sign of peace.

For lack of an official banner to lead the column, the clever fellow also fashioned a primitive flag for us—a jumble of stars, serpents, stripes, and so on. It is a bit crude. Yet it was a jolly good effort, all considered.

"You have talent," I told him recently, sitting together within my tent. "You'd do well with a hat shop, or some such thing, in London."

Outside the open tent flaps the only points of light were the cook-fires. Mosquitoes filled the sticky air. Their whining and the buzzing of other night-time insects made a racket.

For a moment I pictured Virgil and myself together back home, sharing a round of medals, being feted and celebrated, reminiscing as we enjoyed our pipes in the parlour after yet another banquet.

"I want America," he said now.

I could smell the meat roasting on spits as I thought on this.

"Don't be silly. They lack all civility."

"Savages?" he said.

"Indeed."

Our porters grow testy. They argue about the weight of loads, accuse each other of feigning sickness and fatigue. They grow ever more lazy and ungentlemanly.

Consider this incident.

Yesterday, unwilling to get my walking-shoes and feet wet unnecessarily, I commanded one man to bear me on his shoulders across a river. He refused, and I was forced to point my pistol at him. Even as he complied, I feared he might tumble headlong into the current and get us both killed. But faced with an unwanted bullet hole, the man swallowed his pride (and some water, I suspect) and carried me safely.

Later last night, though, he did disappear—along with a bottle of my Madeira. Perhaps I had been unfair to the man.

Today we had another carrier mutilated, hacked to pieces. The donkeys are dead, presumably from the tsetse fly. Our goats have been slaughtered and eaten. The Zanzibaris will not play card games, yet they talk and sing, and drink their banana beer, *pombe*, until late each night.

Other threats abound. Since the rhino is attracted by flame, we face a dilemma now: we have been lighting fires nightly to keep the lions and hyenas away. Now that we are sometimes in the territory of the fire-stomping rhino, do we continue thus?

Again, I save the most bizarre for the last. I refer to our escort of indomitable pluck, Miss Eaton. With each mile we cover, she regresses more to the savage.

While I indulged in tea and biscuits one recent night, the woman invited herself in for a game of Chinese checkers. It quickly became clear she had in mind not checkers but a more physical activity. My camp-cot and tent suffered sorely in the ensuing fracas, and the canvas-clothed structure keeled over in the process. But moral rectitude prevailed.

The next night, my tent flaps whooshed open again. Only an ankle bracelet and patchy coat of red ochre adorned her, and I cast my eyes toward God for help.

"To 'ell with the 'ighway to civilisation," she said, and like a honeymooner, she tugged wildly to undo my belt.

When the woman is in the mood, even a posted guard with rifle and fixed bayonet will not keep her away.

"No need to take yourself so serious," she said with a wink. "Life's meant to include some fun! Being in this boiling sun all day, one needs a break."

It had indeed been a long day of swampy marshes and steep hills, and I scarcely possessed the energy to resist—yet again I did not yield, and eventually drove her outside.

She does have some distinctly attractive physical attributes. Accordingly, I have named the mountain that, lost, we circled for days, "Mount Eaton," on account of its prominent twin peaks. There is something volcanic and mysterious about her, too.

Whether preening from her sidesaddle perch days ago, or bathing before us in full view and calling out to me to scrub her down, the woman talks incessantly. When I remind her of Diogenes' observation that "We all have two ears and one mouth so that we might all listen more and talk less," she rambles on, nonetheless, puzzling aloud over the matter at length.

Lasciviousness and chatter aside, she greatly bolsters our morale.

God help me, does she have me under her spell?

(I do have a confession to share, gentlemen: after her last appearance at my tent in naught but an ankle bracelet, my thoughts of her do wander towards the indiscreet. Oh, the vile thoughts that stain! I have developed masturbatory disease. I can only hope it is temporary, and does not lead to the softening of my brain.)

Today the woman dragged out a mirror much bigger than my own. Sitting on my camp-stool (a snorting rhino destroyed my Morris chair, I should explain), the insect-bitten face that stared back at me seemed that of a stranger. My wide cheekbones bubbled and peeled with sunburn. My auburn hair was stringy and stiff. About my neck, my woollen scarf was a-tatters.

"There's the look of an adventurer in there somewhere," I said, somewhat wryly, to Virgil.

Showers show to the north, hanging like grey towels on a line. I suspect on the morn we will be tromping through mud, and more mud. Even on sunny days, our caravan is a terribly cumbrous thing, so the marching will be difficult. As Commander of the expedition, though, my orders are to relieve Jepson. And I shall.

Murchison, I must beg your pardon. By the number of pages before me, I see I have rambled on. Miss Eaton's babbling must be contagious.

Give my regards to all the anxious, loving hearts in England. Assure them we are men of lofty courage, vigorous resolution, and humble faith.

Yours obediently,<br>
H. R. Huxtable

# LETTER VIII.

*(To G. Jepson, Governour, dated May 1888)*

Jepson—

Do you mock me, sir? True to the bizarre wish stated in your previous letter, our boat, the *Lady Florence*, has sunk in crocodile-infested waters. But we remain undaunted and shall save you yet, despite your rude correspondence.

Yours in potential disgust,

H. R. Huxtable

Commander of the Royal Order of the Muskrat

Jepson Relief Expedition

# LETTER IX.



*(From Mr. Huxtable, addressed to the
news editor of* The London Monitor,
*dated 19 May 1888, Camp Samboozi)*

Dear Mr. Quilby—

How are you, sir? I trust your case of shingles has cleared up
by now. I should dearly hope so. And how are things in foggy
old London? I must ask: has something newsworthy occurred
at Buckingham Palace? I inquire because last eve I had a frightful dream set there: the Queen was thwacking a stunned lackey
with her sceptre. Perhaps it is prescience; perhaps it is nothing.

And perhaps I miss civilisation more than I know. At present
our expedition is hemmed in by blood-thirsty cannibals of the
Baseko tribe. Our survival hangs by a slender thread. Would this
make a good front-page story for your readers?

After steaming up the murky Bambesi, then marching, then
sinking our hand-assembled boat and commandeering dugouts,
we are now past the Po-po rapids. This is still the dangerous

"Land of Look-Behind." Presently, all about us are hills, scraggly trees, and inhospitable savages.

We have somehow missed the stony pass of the Valley of Wild Asses. And for days we have not sighted the local Alps—the newly named Mt. Eaton. I estimate we have now travelled nigh 400 geographical miles.

There is less desolation of the Arabs about here, fewer destroyed villages and panicked refugees. An occasional burned hut or body bound to a tree appears. Yet that is all. Perhaps the Arabs are afraid to engage the cannibals who live in this area—and rightly so, as we recently discovered.

But I get ahead of my tale.

For days, we had put up with a horrid drumming, which Virgil told me indicated that the man-eaters saw meat on the river. They had remained hidden in the bush, however, releasing at their whim an occasional arrow or lance, but always without showing so much as a finger.

Being unable to see them made their presence all the more unnerving, and our own party became tight and nervous. If nothing else, Henry, I am an honest man: I admit some discomfort, too.

"This is dangerous, dangerous," Virgil said one morning. "They come soon."

We were all on high alert. The fear of death showed on many a face.

Recently, on account of the swift river, we had portaged our dugouts again. Now, streaking with perspiration, unnerved by each thump of the distant drums, we advanced into the nearby wood.

Therein, vines and trees fought each other for light. There was scant air to breathe. With trusty rifles at the ready, we painstakingly hewed our path; the challenge was nearly insurmountable. Mosquitoes buzzed about our eyes and ears.

I myself avoided hewing, it being an activity better reserved for those accustomed to such exertions. But I had stepped up to our column's front the better to lead the men. As we climbed a steep, mud-slicked gorge, surrounded by a chaos of vegetation, the heat squeezed in from all sides, and my heart whispered we were going to meet our demise.

Still in the prime of my manhood, I was disinclined to wind up someone's main dish.

To our relief, we found a narrow, partly open path. Moments later, Muffin sidled up to me, his features tense and sharp.

His head turned side to side.

The man did have animal faculties. As I was about to speak, he held up a finger.

"Shh… Quiet."

"What?" I whispered. "I don't hear—"

"Exactly."

Oddly, from above came no birdsong. No screech of monkeys. One could hear only the mosquitoes, angry and impatient.

My throat tightened.

I narrowed my eyes and studied the walls of green around us. Were there any spears or arrows pointed our way? Rioting vegetation was all I could see.

"What think you, Captain?"

"Be lying if I said it don't worry me."

As we pushed onwards, I am sure we all felt the same.

With some trepidation, we advanced—and waited, waited, waited.

Our column bunched up, bumped into each other. The heat pounded against my helmet. Although we grew more worried by the minute, I tried to cheer the men nearest me.

"Courage," I said. "We must be strong as horses, keen as mustard!"

Muffin stared hard at me.

"If you'd like to go well ahead, sir, you could help draw their fire."

One never knows when these fellows are jesting.

The path took an abrupt turn. A moment later I bent down to shake a rock from my walking-shoe. After a slight rustle in the vegetation, a hurtling spear almost passed through one of my belt loops.

The spear lodged in the tree trunk behind me with a terrifying smack. I felt cold at the pit of my stomach.

"Where did—?"

Muffin threw up a hand to indicate a halt.

"Muffin, what—?"

"Ambush!" he cried.

Ahead the trees lay sideways, cut down to obstruct us. My fear welled up and threatened to freeze me.

All at once, with a crescendo of savage whoops, warriors armed with spears, clubs, and bows and arrows swarmed toward us.

"So many!" Muffin said. "We're buggered."

My heart pounded like a steam engine.

The forest came alive with hideous war-cries. Warriors popped up from behind every stone, bush, and tree. Their hair was cut into spirals and zigzags. Ghoulishly, white clay whorls decorated their faces, and their bodies exhibited dots and similarly pagan designs.

At my command, the men—with raised eyebrows, I might add—pitched bright beads into the bush in an attempt to pacify them.

The raging savages would not have them. Apparently they craved our bodies. Quickly they fired off a rain of spears and arrows.

How unfortunate!

"Close ranks!" I shouted, hoping my voice did not quaver.

As the cannibals engaged us, I had an impulse to make judicious use of my heels. Their yells fairly froze the blood in one's veins. Yet I raised my rifle and flung myself into the hottest of the fray.

"For Jepson! And England!"

Arrows whizzed by.

Fighting in the bush like this, we could not make out anything more than a dozen feet ahead of us. We fought with desperate, dare I say gallant, energy. Within the smoke-filled air we fired away at point-blank range. Crack! Crack! Crack! went our rifles. Our bullets shredded brush, snapped branches. One could smell the fear and blood along with the gunpowder.

"Steady, men!" I exhorted. "Steady."

Puffing on a fag by my side, Miss Eaton fired off her revolver. Her movements were calm, intent. She truly was extraordinary.

"Let's send some souls to hell!" Muffin said.

Our shots slashed home. Many enemies fell—yet the others kept coming back. They pressed closer and closer. Amid the flash and din, one charged straight for me, waving a club. Parrot feathers jutted from his hair, and what looked like a snakeskin pouch jounced about his neck. I saw the ferocity on his face.

For a moment I felt helpless.

Then an odd sense of calm settled on me, and I leaped aside, neat as a squirrel. With my rifle butt, I flailed at his head till he collapsed.

It was…It all felt unreal. I wiped the sweat from my brow. Looked around. Captain Muffin yelped as an arrow shaft skewered his arm. Grimacing, he clamped his hand round it as it poured blood.

Near me, a flurry of vicious clubbing dropped two carriers. In return we inflicted a sharp punishment with our Remingtons and Winchesters. Salvo after salvo. An unending crackle of shots and flashes.

"Give them a drubbing, men!" I cried.

One native fell back with a bullet in his forehead. Beside him, another was hit in the throat. The air hissed with bullets. The enemy lay in heaps.

A small hot puff of air passed my cheek. Bloody hell, was that a bullet? Had one of my own men—?

Just who else was the enemy here?

For copious minutes it was touch and go. The cannibals came on in swarms and picked us off, one by one. Captain Muffin was out of action, and who knew where Captain Fuggleby was? Perhaps protecting our supply of spirits? I had to maintain charge.

At my feet a wounded carrier named Hassani blinked desperately, waiting to die. Someone screamed in pain. Closely pursued, an askari blundered desperately through the trees. His attacker fell to my Winchester. It was rather hard to make sense of the chaos. Yet we clearly were wanting of a thicker and more impenetrable defence.

I stared fixedly at the ground.

My mind fumbled for a plan.

As an arrow whizzed past my head, I recalled a military tactic I had gleaned once at the library, while repairing an illustrated volume. I shouted between the trees. Since we were grossly outnumbered, I split our force and ordered one group to provide flanking fire while the other group fell back, then the second group to fire while the first group took a turn retreating further, and so on. This worked perfectly. (As did that library tome's rebinding, I must add.)

"Well done!" I cried, once we were safe enough to stop and take a breath.

Besides our rifles, we had a surprise for the cannibals—sticks of dynamite. I yearned to force them through the forest and into the river with a hearty drive of explosions. To my disappointment, though, they would not stand together and fight in an orderly, civilised manner, like Europeans.

Instead, they hid and fired off an occasional arrow or spear—with grievous results.

We held on.

One askari, ripped through the stomach by a spear, begged that his life be ended. Gently, Miss Eaton placed a hand on his shoulder. With mercy in her grey eyes, she commended the man's soul to "Gawd," aimed her revolver at his brow…and fired.

I desired to say something helpful. I felt the men—and woman—had behaved nobly. Yet what was there to say? As we held there amid the trees, one could almost hear the nerves jangling.

There had been such shedding of blood over so little, briefly I even wondered to what degree we truly were the civilised force here.

Although we could not move forward, eventually our singular little army effected a truce. Through a captive, Virgil arranged a parley at the cannibal village of Zumbo for the day following.

This was only hours prior to my writing, Henry. And if things go ill there, we are soon to meet our demise.

Only minutes ago, Captain Fuggleby thrust his rabid face inside the flap of my tent.

"Truce with savages?" he said. "Pah! It's a trap."

"Captain Fuggleby! Where have you—"

"You blind? You're shoving your head into the tiger's mouth."

With that, he retreated to his own tent. Let me just say: I am anxious as to the morrow.

There is no room for mistakes now.

Yours from cannibal country,<br>
Hubert R. Huxtable, Intrepid Expedition Leader

# LETTER X.



Dear Mr. Quilby—

The ripping tale of our exploits continues!

In retrospect, it may have been unwise yesterday to agree to a parley with man-eaters, yet I know not what choice I had. Captain Fuggleby, tetchy as ever, thinks me barmy. Hindsight is not foreplay, though (or something like that).

"Die, as you wish," he said, when I would not reconsider. "But I ain't going to die with you."

One arm in a sling of Miss Eaton's contrivance, Captain Muffin refused to accompany us to the parley, as well. (Apparently, the poison in his wound was old, or her cleansing of it with permanganate of potash was effective, or both: he survived.)

Brave Miss Eaton insisted on attending.

(After further explication, you—and your newspaper readers—may think my own conduct also rather brave. Although I am a humble man, I confess I cannot deny it.)

At midday today a pinched-looking native strode into our camp to lead us to the cannibal village. He wore little more than a bow and quiver.

Before we departed, Captain Muffin surprised me by requesting to shake hands. As we did so, we both knew we might never see each other again.

"Ain't spoke well of you," he said, with a rough sideways smile. "Truth to tell, I've dropped some venom on you. Might've called you a fool, a ninny—"

"That's enough, sir."

"A git as well." His red-rimmed eyes studied my face as if to confirm his assessment, and he gave a low chuckle. "And a worthless clown."

"Truly, that's—"

"A plonker? Uh-huh, that, too… Anyhow, good luck."

"You've proven yourself quite something, Captain Muffin."

Fuggleby shook a grimy finger at Muffin. His frown made clear his annoyance.

"Arse kisser!" he said.

Muffin promptly tackled him and the fists began to fly.

"Gentlemen!" I said. "Cease this tomfoolery! Save your energies for the cannibals."

Our guide scratched his chin with his thumb, then whisked Miss Eaton, Virgil, and me away.

"You'll just cock things up!" Fuggleby called, by way of farewell.

Our little party was shielded only by Providence and ten heavily armed askaris. Yet I, at least outwardly, was confident.

Any other attitude would have meant admitting our doom.

Our guide sped along a winding path. As the rest of us picked our way through the roots underfoot, he would not talk. Occasionally he gestured with a finger or grunt, dour as an aged Parliament member. When I tried to explain I was nearly an agent of the British government myself and should be treated as such, he appeared unimpressed.

Perhaps he did not understand.

As we drew closer to the cannibal village, our brows knotted in worry. Drums beat to sound our approach.

Virgil rubbed a hand over his head, his face grave.

"We maybe die today."

Something large crashed about in the trees, and the heat hammered at us. My throat felt parched. I sought a casual response to demonstrate my lack of fear, yet none came to mind.

"Might this parley help?" I said at last.

Virgil considered my question a moment.

"No. Now, I do not think so. We have bad situation."

I sighed.

"You're not terribly inspiring, my good chap."

Before we sighted the village, our guide told Virgil that our party had to don the animal-skin blindfolds he had been clutching.

"Oh my," Miss Eaton said.

Need I say we hesitated at first, Henry, more than a tad concerned? (Specially the askaris, for what good are soldiers without vision?)

Afraid we were about to disappear into thin air, we had a stalemate there on the outskirts of Zumbo.

Our guide stomped his bare feet and threw a tantrum while we held our own little parley off to one side.

Eventually, we gave in—trusting to occasional sneak-peeks. We joined hands, as much for moral support as to keep ourselves steady, and without tripping up too much, moved cautiously into the village.

As our guide began to remove our blindfolds, I swallowed hard. It had been an edgy night and morn. Now the wait was over.

When my blindfold came off, I took in my breath sharply.

Inside a stockade ringed with cone-shaped huts, blood-thirsting savages positively surrounded us.

"Sweet Jesus," I said softly. "Sweet Jesus."

Was this parley going to prove foolhardy? Had I opened a sack of snakes? How fervently I wished for some slugs of my trusty Mrs. Winslow's Soothing Syrup!

Well, I told myself, best foot forward. Get on with it.

No large cook-pots bubbled before us, which was at least a source of relief.

At first we received only a grand, concentrated stare. Men and women nearly innocent of clothing, dusky children, a few barking curs—all gave us the once-over. More than one sized up my body parts, I imagined.

Sweat rolled down my cheeks like tears. Miss Eaton hung on me for support, her eyes wide, more timid than I had ever seen her.

The askaris fingered their rifles.

Little Virgil broke the spell, tugging on my sleeve.

"We die here for England?"

"Perhaps," I said. "Indeed. Now, it's necks or nothing."

Mentally I reviewed every tome I had ever read on Africa, exploration, and etiquette for the proper manner of assembling with cannibals. None seemed to have covered the subject sufficiently, so I would have to improvise. (Perhaps I shall write a book on the topic myself when I return to England.)

I nodded to the crowd and mumbled the salutation "Kina Bomba."

For added effect (and to loosen the soil packed on my trousers from tumbling on the path), I shook an already shaky leg. In return, the native welcoming committee gnashed their teeth and slashed the air with their spears.

As the crowd muttered and grimaced, a man with hair plaited into a horn stalked up to me. He waved a big knob club. My mouth hung open in fear as the man threw dirt in my face.

"Local hello," Virgil said.

After discreetly spitting the soil from my mouth, I stooped to scoop up a handful of earth and returned the salutation.

"Greetings, one and all," I said.

We were led past the sole shade-tree towards a long hut. There we were to meet with Ringi, the chieftain. An elephant roared outside the stockade.

The askaris could not keep their eyes off the tattooed native belles. I had to admit that, for cannibals, they were quite shapely. Their scanty clothing consisted of only some cotton here and a little bark there. If we survived, I knew this fashion statement would be sure to inspire Miss Eaton.

Did I mention the heat, Henry?

Human skulls hung outside the palaver hut, which was also painted with snakes and devils. Though this filled me with dread, the sun was so strong I was anxious to enter and escape the heat.

Inside, it was dim but for the immediate circle of light about a flickering fire. Even in the low light, though, I was able to make out an imposing presence. Horribly obese and one-eyed, Ringi looked up from his stool. Scars scored his swollen face. On his fat head sat a cap of leopard fur and a tiara of the same beast's claws. On his body hung a tunic; it gleamed with bands of gold. Though we were out of the sun, a heavily decorated sort of umbrella was held above his head.

His feather-head-dressed captains squatted on their heels about him. Unseen drummers and rattlers carried on in the dark.

He did not move.

When I gave him a polite dip of my chin, he merely looked us over with an imperious air.

Unsure how to proceed, I wondered if I ought to throw dirt in his face, but I decided against it. After coughing nervously, I let loose with a kind of modified salaam.

"Greetings from the leader of the Royal Order of the Muskrat Jepson Relief Mission," I said. "How do you do, sir?"

The almost spherical savage cyclops sat mute.

His men shifted positions so we might move nearer to him. Our party sat on wood stools. To one side of me, Miss Eaton stared at the sling of jawbones hanging across his shoulder and apparently did not feel like talking herself.

The chief would not shake my proffered hand. Instead, he sat there waving a bunch of animal tails between us—likely part of some black and dangerous art.

Eventually he opened his mouth. His teeth ended in hideously sharp points. The sight of them brought the blood into my cheeks.

Would it be any more frightening to sit with the devil himself?

When he patted his belly, we were unsure whether he anticipated the delight of eating us or was asking for something to eat.

Quickly we scrounged up among us a few pieces of toffee, somewhat the worse for our travels. Just as quickly he chomped them down. Head held high, he demanded another for his pet chimpanzee. This chimp wore a tiny leopard cap, too.

The chief signalled his drummers and rattlers to tone down their racket, then finally asked through our versatile linguist, Virgil, whether our party was after ivory or slaves.

"We come for Jepson," I said.

"What is this Jepson?" Ringi asked.

I did my best to tell him. I explained we merely wished to travel through—and quickly out of—his country.

When I adjusted my spectacles and asked if he had seen our twisted wisps of grass, he merely laughed. He then indicated for his musicians to resume with their noise, and afterwards an old man with clouded eyes whispered into his ear.

"We must eat," Ringi then proclaimed.

I cannot speak for my companions, but for me this statement brought my heart nearly into my mouth.

Fortunately, he did not mean what I had feared.

With a clap of his hands, a pair of nubile belles presented heaping bowls of manioc and roast meat. Relieved though I was that we were not to be the meal, I hoped the meat was not human.

Apparently he is not impressed with the Arabs. Speaking through Virgil while stuffing his face, he touched on their atrocities and said that for this reason he had recently moved his village to its hidden location in dense thorn bush and trees.

He would not exchange blood with them and thus make peace, he said. Nor would he let them take a wife from his tribe. As I stared at his teeth in fascination, he said many of the skulls hanging outside had been slavers. Quickly I explained that an occasional unprincipled outsider should not lead him to condemn us all.

At that point, Miss Eaton lit a cigarette.

She smoothed the hem of her dress and whispered to me: "Strength. You must present as a bricky sort."

I gave her the briefest of nods.

Turning back to Ringi, I said, "Chief, we have brass wire, cloth, and beads for taxes to pass through your land."

At first, mumbling to one of his captains, he would have none of it.

Apparently, though, he knew of our dynamite's power, and he found himself in a quandary. Perhaps to make me fear his strength, too, he spoke of his own power.

At his signal, a native with cropped ears and lopped-off hands popped in. When the poor man struck his cheeks with the stumps of his wrists, I shuddered. Ringi said this was what happened to men who wronged him.

He looked me threateningly in the eye. He pulled out a long obsidian dagger and explained with it his method of dissecting men.

His manner was so convincing, my stomach began to feel rather unsettled.

One thought ran through my mind, Henry: *I wanted to see Africa untouched by modern influence, and here I am—yet therefore I am going to be cut up like a beefsteak and devoured.*

Ringi looked pointedly at his knife, then at me.

Given my tested fortitude as a librarian, I imagine I looked a paradigm of calm concentration. Inside, though…

Crikey!

Last night, for reasons I imagine are obvious, I had not rested well. Thus my first, unintentional, response to this threat now was an immense yawn. This seemed to impress Ringi and his men somewhat.

The askaris had sat silent. Now, one of them demanded that we leave and come back in full force to burn the place down.

I blew out a breath and shook my head.

"Patience."

They murmured tensely. Then I did something rash. Possibly brave.

I stared at Ringi hard. I stomped my foot.

"Put that dagger away, before I"—I demonstrated a fist—"box your ears. You'll not disrespect the Crown." Never before had my voice sounded so strong and composed. "Cross us any further and you'll regret it. The savage who can kill me has not been born. Hubert Reginald Huxtable has spoken!"

Everything stopped suddenly, as if by magic. Even the drumming.

Virgil glanced at me, then at Ringi, blinked slowly, and translated.

Every eye in the hut was on me. The askaris thumped their rifle butts on the ground in approbation.

Ringi looked surprised.

After a moment of indecision, he put his blade away. Relief washed through me.

"We must drink!" he said.

The chief offered up more pombe than could ever have filled even my captains' stomachs. After such trials, the drink was more than welcome.

Once I had quaffed two bowls down, the smoky room spun. If offered a fire-walking ceremony to participate in, I would have been happy to do so. The spirits also helped the askaris ease up; Virgil appeared to relax, too.

With the drinking, Ringi grew more curious. He inquired about my field glasses, whether they hung round my neck in decoration or marked my status as leader. As I handed them to him, I explained their purpose. He scanned the dusky room, magnifying those in his field of vision with wonderment.

"Strong magic!"

For a while he would not give them back.

With the drinks, he also grew greatly impressed by Miss Eaton's skin. He felt the hem of her dress and pointed at her calf.

"White all over? White all over?"

He had never seen a woman such as this, he stated. He now appeared highly interested and said that if some of her upper front teeth were knocked out, she would appear even more desirable.

She bit her lip shut but gave a peculiar smile: I was unsure whether his attentions thrilled her or terrified her. Yet she would not look him in the eye.

Positively ignoring me, his leopard-skin-capped head held lower now, he told her he should like to take her for his seventh wife.

"Nah, nah, nah, that'll never do," she said, with a huffing sound. She made a quick reassuring touch to her coiffure. "Could never wed you and break the 'earts of so many others."

(The woman says she used to run a school for wayward girls, Henry. I am still not certain whether she took them in or trained them to be wayward.)

Given her refusal, he shrugged and was silent for some moments, presumably searching for another scheme to cement our friendship. For then, he proposed that he and I engage in a blood exchange.

I knew I must accept—to refuse would likely be a grievous insult.

Do not think me a savage, Henry; it is the local custom. And before I even knew where I was off to, two giggly maidens with copper necklaces caressing their bare bosoms escorted me off to dress for the ceremony.

I suspected the portly Don Juan at least partly wanted me gone so he might further his advances towards Miss Eaton. So I looked back at her in concern.

"I can manage!" she said brightly.

I had no real complaints at the time, hustled off to be prepared by the two belles. I knew nothing about typical cannibal ceremony. Yet I did know that my own clothes were covered with dirt. And I am afraid I smelled pungent besides.

I soon returned, surprisingly refreshed and dressed in a cowrie-shell necklace and a single piece of woven-bark cloth—its two corners tied in a knot over one shoulder and passing under the opposite armpit. The cloth had been dyed to look like a leopard skin. The garment left one side of my body partly exposed, and it flapped about so, it bordered on indecent.

Many in the room chuckled at my entrance—Huxtable gone native, Florence's ragged scarf about my neck yet. Miss Eaton, however, seemed to approve.

The actual blood-letting itself proved brief, causing little pain. As the incisions were cut and blood exchanged, I did not flinch. We then heard from the native orchestra again, a regular hubbub.

Yet for the bloody part, Henry, the ceremony bore a striking resemblance to a Muskrat Lodge induction.

After the ceremony, Ringi grew cranky, again testing my nerves.

His gaze uncertain, as if he saw double (or single, being one-eyed), and apropos of nothing, he yelled, "You can't kill us all!"

I assured him we would rather make peace with his people than kill them, which seemed to mollify him somewhat.

He inquired about our beads and cloth. Though he suspected we had the power of more dynamite, the man clearly sought some right-of-way tolls. He demanded we cater to what amounted to a regular Christmas list.

At his command, men popped into the room with three huge baskets. We were to fill them with presents of gunpowder, candy, a captain's coat, British tobacco…The list went on.

Much more concerning, I noted that the one exit had been blocked off by a squad of savages and felt our only recourse lay in decisive action. I stood, summoning up my most commanding look and tone of voice.

"This is no way to treat your blood-brother! Is your head full of bunkum? If you're seeking peace, you've proceeded in an—an ill-mannered fashion."

Miss Eaton reached out and squeezed one of my buttocks in support.

"Nonetheless," I said, seeking a way forward that would allow Ringi to preserve his status, "we're happy to provide gifts in token of our friendship."

I promised him a wealth of fine beads, cloth, wire, a canvas-covered camp-stool, and more toffee. Smoke in my eyes and still feeling tipsy from the pombe, I think I even went so far as to promise a thundershower for his crops.

Throughout my speech he stared fixedly at the ringlets of Miss Eaton's hair, and as I finished he kissed her hand.

But then a furrow appeared between his brows, and his eyes turned to hard green nuggets. Turning to me, he burst out with a statement that made Virgil visibly tense.

Anxiously, I waited for the translation.

"He say, 'This woman is mine! Or I will make your skulls into cups for drink.'"

(Up until that last comment, Henry, I had been of the general belief that, besides their man-eating propensities, and forgiving the occasional liquor-induced outburst, the cannibals were a people with good manners.)

Another tension-filled moment passed, then Miss Eaton clicked her tongue in disapproval.

"Oh dear, that'll never do, mate," she said, shaking her head.

Few have borne the responsibility I did at that moment.

After a hiccup, I added, "I should say not! You are barmy, sir."

"We must go," Virgil said, urgently tugging at my bark-cloth garb.

The askaris cocked their rifles.

The cannibals drew their spears and raised their clubs.

Would I find myself embroiled in a duel for the lady? I was considering suggesting pistols at ten paces when Ringi shouted that we had a day to consider his proposal.

If we refused, he said, perhaps he would make me into a stew. Or perhaps he would have me bound to a tree and spears thrust at me. He then would have my head cut off and my limbs scattered about for the hyenas.

We had little temptation to loiter further in Zumbo.

With weapons drawn, we readied to leave, prepared to force our way if necessary. I straightened my shoulders, looked him in his one eye.

"Leave us be! Or…we'll make the devils in our guns come out!" His men backed away, though their weapons remained raised. "All right, then, we shall be getting on." I gave Ringi a courteous nod. "Good day to you."

Hastily, we put a significant distance between us and Zumbo.

As we paused a moment to catch our breath, I realised I had left my trousers, flannel undergarments, and jacket behind.

Virgil said, "At least we did not leave our heads, too."

Miss Eaton stared down as the hem of my new garment slipped aside from my hips.

"Watch where you keep your eyes, Miss Eaton," I said.

"Oh, Mr. 'uxtable." She chortled. "Too late for that!"

It eased my mind a moment to laugh along with her.

We huffed and puffed our way down the winding path. As we scrambled across rock-strewn rapids, the light began to change with the sun's descent.

Fortune soon shone upon us, in the form of a black-dirt trail gouged by elephants. It brought us almost directly to our main party, who were halted on another path amidst the great green height of the forest.

Never had I been so glad to see Fuggleby's ruddy, scowling mug.

Before I could sputter anything intelligible, he screwed up his eyes and examined my leopard-print robe. There was a sheen of sweat on his face. He smirked.

"We built us a hasty stockade, made bandages, rolled pills. Got us a goodly number of rounds per rifle, and ain't about to jump into any cook-pots!"

I could have bussed him.

"Jolly good."

"What in blazes you been up to? A bloody costume party?"

Not long afterwards, we recounted the harrowing tale as we refreshed ourselves with tea. I fancy I did not imagine the look of respect which threatened to make an appearance on my captains' faces.

We hear the talking drums of the cannibals yet, Henry.

We possess no more dynamite. Still, we do have gunpowder and our wits. To withdraw would be pusillanimous, but we may find a slight retreat to be tactically sound. There are traps filled with barbed skewers about, which makes movement by night specially dangerous—yet we may need to risk it rather than await another barbarous assault.

Blood still seeping through his wrapped wound, Captain Muffin agreed.

"As one knackered eye said to the other, let's pack our bags and leave."

Of course Captain Fuggleby, looking mean and bothered, felt otherwise.

"Ain't right to run off. Let's fight them and be done with it. Their chief needs a smacking. We'll pour death and damnation on them." His face had turned purple. He growled incoherently. "Oh, we'll let the daylight into them! I almost pity the buggers."

Muffin spat at Fuggleby's feet.

"Ah, you couldn't beat me granny."

Like a couple of cross, circling dogs, they exchanged glares. Surely one of them was about to get their teeth loosened.

"You know who runs?" Fuggleby shouted back. "Only little rabbits run!"

"Captains!" I said wearily, breaking them up for what felt like the ten-thousandth time.

Some of the askaris may not be seasoned soldiers after all, either. In battle yesterday they had fired recklessly; one broke ranks and ran. Now, they whine that they do not want to die. The carriers have begun praying to their heathen deity. The wounded express fear of being left behind.

It would not be an exaggeration to say there is more than a touch of tension in camp.

Do we attack? Would that not just delay us further—assuming we are even victorious? Yet if we do not go on the offensive, we may merely be postponing an inevitable assault on our own party. We have our work cut out, I can tell you. Retreat or not, though, I will not simply relinquish my skull. And one way or another, I suspect we shall have a proper scrap before all is said and done.

"We need to patrol," I said at last to all. "Vigorously. Then determine if we even have a chance at escape. We're still alive and on two feet, and I have every intention of keeping it that way."

May a courier live to bring you this correspondence. If so, I hope you find it of sufficient interest to print.

I will write again. That is, unless my head is cut off and my limbs scattered about for the hyenas.

Yours humbly,
Hubert R. Huxtable

# LETTER XI.

*(To Mrs. Phineas M. Ackley Boggs,*
*London, dated ? May 1888)*

Mrs. Boggs—

Do you remember me, ma'am? (Do you remember anything? I should hope not.) Do you teach, still? I endured your Standard V class once—or twice, truth be told—and you oft predicted I would come to no good. Unfairly, you referred to me as "short on brains." True, I did pretend to read at first by memorising a few sentences. Who knew you would finally note my book was upside-down? (Later, it did turn out that I was in need of spectacles.)

Well, I am in the wilds of Africa now, and I prove you wrong. I sit not under a cardboard dunce cap anymore, but on a campstool helmeted under the great outdoors.

I am something of a hero, as it happens.

Our caravan marches through swamps and jungle, through brush and tall mazes of bamboo. Incisions are cut on my tan arms by cannibals, and I flinch not. Not much, anyway. When they attack with barbed spears and arrows, I rally our force with gusto.

You caned me once for holding my pen out of style. Alas, nothing nice ever seemed to happen in your draughty classroom.

From the schoolyard, I do remember one chant: "Eaver weaver, chimney sweeper / had a wife and couldn't keep her / had another, didn't love her / up the chimney he did shove her." If only we could have shoved you up a chimney, ma'am.

Goodbye: I seek a life of the grand manner. We blaze a glorious path through unknown lands.

Yours Sincerely,
Hubert Reginald Huxtable

# LETTER XII.

*(From Commander Huxtable to the Jepson
Relief Committee, dated 28 May 1888, from
Tele Island, the Ibumi River or Tanga River)*

Dear Chairman—

Heavens, where do I begin?

When I stop to think, I begin to worry, and the more I worry, the more my stomach ails me. I think my insides hate me. Some days here in the wilderness I could not survive without my laudanum-infused tonic, Mrs. Winslow's Soothing Syrup.

We have beached our dugouts and cleared the brush at Tele Island and will rest here. I have draped my stockings on my helmet to dry. I have lacked time lately for bird-watching or the chase of Lepidoptera. The surly tribes of the Land of Look-Behind have seen to that.

This is a strange place, Murchison. There are different realities here.

Such as one-eyed cannibals as big as my Aunt Edna. (Both are cantankerous murderers, too, come to think of it.)

After an initial skirmish on 19 May, the day following we parleyed with the cannibals of Zumbo. Despite my imposing bearing and keen diplomatic abilities, we barely escaped with our lives. Their chief, Ringi, cunning as the leopard whose skin he wears on his head, meant to have us for dinner, I think—not as guests, but as the entrée.

We beat a hasty retreat, their drums again calling the assembly.

Perhaps I did not duly impress the white man's greatness on them?

With a push to the Samboozi River, our force again sent bullets through the brutes' heads. Like locusts, they followed in close proximity. While courageously bringing up the rear so as to allow the others to escape, I stumbled to the ground. As I arose, I found myself well on the way to meet my Maker.

A horde of savages licked their chops as they moved in for the kill. The sight sent a ripple of fear down my spine.

But for my one bullet and my rifle, Murchison, I was entirely alone.

Only a few feet away, the forest rose in a green wall of leaves and snaky vines. Could I dash into it before being unkindly pierced by arrows?

"Dear Lord," I said to myself.

But making a show of defiance, I shook my fist in their direction.

To my great surprise and pleasure, they immediately bolted away. Soon after, though, to my great surprise and displeasure, came a loud roaring from behind me. A hungry-looking lion just about tapped me on my shaking shoulder. Apparently he also intended me to be his dinner guest.

For a moment I stood rigid, terrified, helpless. The sweat came out afresh on my forehead.

Raising my rifle and taking careful aim, I squeezed off my last shot.

I did not hit the beast—but I did succeed in scaring him off. He and my other pursuers were gone.

I took deep breaths to calm myself. And before long I broke into a grin and gave a restrained whoop.

"Three cheers to that," I said. "Remarkable."

(Someone is watching out for me, I think, Murchison. If so, I wish he might watch a tad closer and make the general going easier.)

I suppose I should not complain, on the other hand. I shall never forget the horrid look of one of Ringi's mutilated subjects. His ears had been cropped and his hands lopped off due to his chief's barbarities. That—or worse—might have been my fate.

I did not leave any body parts behind in Zumbo. Yet I did leave my last change of trousers and jacket in a serpent-decorated hut. Fortunately, I have taken a liking to the imitation leopard-skin bark-fibre robe I departed in. Though perhaps a bit indecent in look, it is a cool and highly rugged garment.

I soon found the others. Huffing up and down hill after hill, we left Ringi and his filed teeth behind us.

The danger thus diminished, I dared hope.

Captain Muffin disagreed.

In fact, the rascal has gone off his head and deserted us.

Not long after our escape, he and I had stood to one side during a halt. Suddenly he began to mutter. He stamped a foot. Face marred with bug-bites, eyes wild, he yelled that he was going to leave our caravan.

"You drunken fool," I said. "We have a mission."

Vehemently, he shook his head. He had the look of a baited wolf which snarls and bites over its shoulder.

"I tell you, my mind is all out o' order! Blimey, I…" He grimaced. "I'm sick of all of youse."

"You're making a mistake. A grave one."

"Bugger off!"

"Chin up, Captain. You're just—"

"This mission? It smells. It stinks!"

I considered threatening him, to prevent other desertions as well as his own, yet could I rightfully pull my Webley on someone in such a disarranged state? (Clearly, Mr. Chairman, the lamps were on, but no-one was at home.)

Mosquitoes whined round my head as I deliberated.

Finally I said, "If you love your country, sir, if you're a patriot, you won't—"

"Kiss me arse," he said, and bolted into the bush, mad as a bag of ferrets.

Despite myself, I called out, feeling in that moment that our differences no longer mattered.

"Fare thee well, Captain Muffin! I would advise you to be wary."

I wished him luck. I did. For this trekking into Earth's darkest regions is not for the anaemic-minded, sane or no, and in a way I suppose I shall miss the bloody fool. Fuggleby does, I gather. He is now left with no partner for carousing and fighting with.

We have lost a certain symmetry.

In truth, when later that day I informed Fuggleby of Muffin's unsettling departure, he teared up. For a while he was silent as we marched on. Afterwards, apparently he felt compelled to share a memory or two.

His face still looked frightful from his recent go-around with Muffin. A purple welt underscored one eye.

"Well, hope he don't fall in no pit."

"What do—"

"He told me his pa died after falling down a mineshaft, when well in his cups. Happens, right?"

I stopped a moment to dab my brow and shrugged.

"Well, I—"

"Think on the rest, though!" We strode on between streaming vines and swirls of purple butterflies. Overhead, monkeys clambered in the branches. "Muffin's ma, too. And his brothers—all fell down stairs and mineshafts!" He made a little sound in his mouth. "Guess they all liked a nip now and then—"

"I get the picture, Captain."

"Could soak the stuff up. Said they even drank turpentine…. Oh my, he could throw out a fist, though."

I swatted at a huge hornet menacing my face.

"Thank you for the touching—"

"Turpentine! That'd give a twist to your innards." He grinned oddly and gave me a look as if he would not mind if I plunged down a mineshaft myself. His voice took on a threatening edge. "Ah, the things some will sink to."

That look!

Did the fool blame me for Muffin's departure? Did he blame me for every shortcoming of our mission? The unbearable heat? The clouds of insects? The man-eaters?

During our battle with the cannibals, someone had fired a bullet past my head. Had that been him?

The brute, like my own twisted-up stomach, worried me.

"Indeed," I finally said. "All I know is, he'll find no gin-shops in the bush."

My instincts served me right, Murchison—for soon it did turn out that this was my time for further captain troubles.

For the past weeks, we have had carrier difficulties, I should note. A short while ago, despite their reluctance, at the sounding of the horn the men turned to their bales and began to march off in a sullen silence.

"We're many days behind schedule," I called after them. "We must push." I clapped my hands. "Toleka, toleka! Chop, chop. We must shoot forward like arrows, like cheetahs, like… something else fast. Forward, always forward! We must make a beeline for Fort Bim—no lying around, scratching our bellies."

"What a blowhard," Fuggleby said, with one of his best sneers.

"That's enough, Captain. Now, where was I…?" My crack force and I had just over thirty days to meet our deadline. In my mind I turned over an hourglass. Thirty days! "Forward! This is a march, not a stroll. Double-time. Triple-time. We must away!"

I remained behind to drive any stragglers on.

Fuggleby soon brought the caravan to a halt. Despite our need for haste, I had also chastised him earlier for whacking porters on the shoulders with a stout stick; he had appeared to derive enjoyment from the beatings. The scene had made me want to give him a ruddy good hiding.

"Thank you for your wise counsel," he had said then, yet he had looked ready to raise that stout stick to me.

So I had said, "Need I signal for a muster of all soldiers on the double with their weapons?"

(The rascal likely also had been leading the caravan's mumble-mumble against me.)

He had backed off, then. Now, with this halt, what was he up to?

On a sandy trail edged by towering elephant grass, he stepped towards me with angry gesticulation. We had no company, and when he pulled out and readied his pistol, my heart skipped a beat.

His neck sinews stood taut. The things some will sink to, indeed! Despite the squirm of fear in my belly, I stiffened my spine and looked at him with displeasure.

"Lower that weapon," I said firmly.

He would not.

"I ain't no football, and I don't deserve a kicking," he said.

I surmised he needed a new fighting partner. Or had he been into some turpentine himself? I glanced about for a lion to save me. There was none, so I drew my Webley and pointed it.

"You, sir, are—are unmannerly. Comport yourself."

"Pah!"

"This is no rough oyster-saloon! May I remind you you've signed an agreement, committed yourself to our party's harmony?"

"You ain't no leader."

"Have you been plotting against—"

"Mr. Big Man, ain't you? O Great One! Cracked as your spectacles."

"Captain, you're the one acting foolishly."

"An all-round jackass."

His grimy finger rested on his pistol's trigger. Would he actually fire on me? Why not? For what was one more sin to a man so steeped in transgression?

"Don't be rash," I said. "Do as I…"

My voice trailed off as he turned. A flock of green ibises trumpeted by. Apparently that had caught his attention.

No.

Out of the high grass surged Miss Eaton.

"Nah, nah, nah," she said.

Never had her nasal tones sounded so lovely. Her Adams revolver pointed at Fuggleby's head. Virgil stood by her, his long blowgun poised.

"'old on, Captain," she added. "Don't think I'd put an 'ole in you? If you're going to force this, no-one gives a toss what 'appens to you."

He breathed out heavily, like an angry bull.

"Lay down your weapon, Fuggleby," I said. "Open your eyes here."

We stared in silence at one another for a few tense seconds.

A moment later his face sank, and he lowered his pistol.

"This heat? Brings out the savage, eh, Huxtable? Apologies. Perhaps I need me another drink." He scratched inelegantly under his arm and smacked his lips. "I've a powerful thirst on me."

"Well, then…. We'll talk later. I have no fear of you—remember that." I knew I should further impress my authority. "And I dare say we have plentiful good hanging trees hereabouts."

"Mercy me, ain't you the wisest, noblest—"

"Do not mock me, Captain. That will be all."

He gave me an overly sweet smile and departed, presumably to further imbibe.

"Well done." I nodded to Miss Eaton and Virgil and touched my heart in thanks. "Maybe things'll quiet down now."

"The quiet pool is where the crocodile lives," Virgil said.

As usual, his comment hit the target. Miss Eaton and he had helped save me and our mission then—but what about the next time?

So, we have lost Captain Muffin, and Captain Fuggleby is a clear threat—a snake in the grass that needs to be dealt with.

Fortunately though, shortly after that close encounter, our caravan gained another officer: Lieutenant Ross Taubman Potter, a real dandified fellow. Potter and his young manservant, Dovey, staggered into our camp not long ago, dreadful wrecks, looking half-starved and fully unwashed.

"Heavens!" Lieutenant Potter said upon seeing us.

With great enthusiasm he shook my hand. He was all made up like a rather wicked though rough-worn buccaneer.

"A pleasure to meet you, sir," I said.

"Thought we'd never set our peepers on Englishmen again."

I looked over his silk scarf and tattered tight trousers. Remnants of lavish silver piping decorated his red tailcoat. Likely, he wondered about my own costume. Perhaps he coveted my cowrie-shell necklace? He wore a remnant of face paint on one eyelid, and yet I liked him right away.

He had clear-cut features. His hair was parted on the right, and a long forelock fell over one eye.

With a wink, he turned to our Miss Eaton. Behind him the slanting sun glittered on the trees.

"And how is every little thing with you, ma'am?"

She lifted her sun helmet in greeting and pulled out her cigarettes.

"Fancy one?"

"Good God, an Ogden's Guinea Gold?" He rubbed his hands together with joy. "That's dear of you! Please."

In a moment light grey smoke clouded the air.

Upon closer examination, Potter and his boy looked half ready for the vultures. We had heard of another British force in the area and were gravely sorry to learn that they were the sole survivors. When pressed as to their own misfortunes, they put on forlorn faces and mumbled about a hair-breadth escape and many tragic scenes.

I told him we had met with and engaged the cannibals in battle, and he was amazed we had survived, too. Apparently he and his small contingent were headed to a trading station downriver when ambuscaded themselves. Potter had suffered an arrow wound about his heart; when he broke out the story, he readily raised his shirt and showed his scar.

"Take a look. It heals yet."

"No need to disrobe further," I said.

Interestingly enough, the man carries an intercepted packet, Murchison: communications from Jepson to Sheik Amin Ali Ibid. Though they are scribed in Arabic, and therefore presently undecipherable (our porters lack reading), I cannot help but wonder if Jepson himself may have dirtied his hands in the ivory or slave trade. Yet perhaps I do him a disservice, and there is another explanation for the packet.

We shall see.

Fuggleby dislikes Potter, and groans each time the lieutenant, hands on hips, gives him an order. I gather he feels threatened by a Mary Jane. Then again, he dislikes everyone, and groans when I order him about as well.

Lately I have been troubled by fever. For days I shivered in the brutal heat, weak and queasy. I forgot names and days. I saw faces in the trees and sky. Dreams of Miss Hoople and her beady blue eyes tormented me. In my feverish mind I carved bold letters into an acacia tree's trunk: "WE MUST SAVE JEPSON!" My every joint felt swollen, and my head felt as if it would split open.

Given our lack of quinine, I ate a whole tin of Enos Liver salts. Virgil also fed me cinchona bark. Yet my body refused to settle. The men bore me forward in a litter.

Drained and beaten with the fever, I yearned not to be here, yearned not to be sick. Why had I ever considered leading this ill-fated mission?

My teeth chattered. I moaned.

Was I about to enter eternity? This I knew not.

Fuggleby insisted on covering me with a bunch of broad leaves as protection from the sun. Perhaps he and the men did not want to see my blistered skin or hear my muffled complaints.

Finally, he leaned over my litter and spat as if something was stuck to his tongue.

"Know what could help?" he said. "A hot dung poultice on your forehead."

Only now am I able to write and read without the print blurring. Only now have I been able to shave the growth of beard from my face. I shall soak in the sulphur spring just off the river's bank on the morrow. The warm, muddy sediment is said to have curative properties.

I hope I can slip in without attracting Miss Eaton's attentions. The woman carries a hippo-hide whip. The mere thought makes me whimper.

Many of us are already lamed with ulcerated lesions, and we sorely lack the balms our cowardly physician made off with. The tiniest wound can fester into an ulcer here. The terrain also ensures that our shoes fall to pieces.

We move about, nonetheless, marching or paddling from one rapid to another. (I am getting better with my direction-finding, yet I still wish the parallels and meridians were marked around here.) The Tanga or Ibumi—whichever it is—is more of a creek than a true river hereabouts. We are walled in by lofty, monkey-gambolled hills. But we have had enough of tumultuous rivers.

We constantly watch for more cannibals. Along with them and Fuggleby, I am also keeping my eye on the Zanzibaris, who continue to mutter.

I may be rapidly using up my nine lives.

Almost a fortnight ago, while out stalking wildflowers, again I nearly met my Maker. A porter suddenly keeled over very dead beside me. (Alas, my book on local flora was muddied in the process.)

The man had been felled by a poison dart in the forehead. Had the dart felled the wrong man? Was I the intended target? And if so, was I spared through Providence or luck? Perhaps if the man had believed in the Christian God, he might not have fallen victim either.

As for the culprit, nearly everyone is suspect. Unbeknownst to Virgil, the only person I wholly trust, someone had borrowed his blowgun and darts while he napped. I nearly died in his sleep.

As mentioned before, I am not overly popular among the carriers. Adversity may not bring out the best in all of us. There is resentment over the issue of standard-bearing. For a while, we lost our standard-bearers to the savages at a horrid pace. This job, therefore, is not sought after, specially as these Zanzibaris fail to understand the vital importance of leading our marches with a banner. They call me chicken-hearted because I bring up the rear of the column. They also laugh at my pith helmet draped with bug netting.

I have handed out tin Royal Order of the Muskrat medals, thinking to impress them with the greatness of our mission, but they merely use them to hold their turbans together.

Some of the men have snuck off with their loads in the night.

Unlike those turbans, our force is unravelling.

Like a fresh wind (or hurricane), Miss Eaton tries to cheer us with song and pantomime. Sometimes it seems to be woman's office to preserve the saintly impulses which redeem our fallen state.

She also demonstrates naughty whip tricks for us. Still, she can get little clapping from the men.

"Perhaps they merely like their own songs and dances," I said to her. "I suspect one can't force fun."

Lieutenant Potter enjoys it all, anyway. Sitting about, combing his thick locks with his hand, the man reminds me of a flamboyant flamingo.

"I miss my Beethoven," he said one recent afternoon. "And good God could I go for some rock candy!"

All I could give him was a shrug.

"Our last sweets went to a cannibal chief."

He is appreciated by most as being sensible and good-natured, despite his dandified ways. I trust him and Virgil to keep me apprised of any further murmurs of discontent.

We are not getting fat, and presently I would do most anything for a slab of good cheddar. Some days we eat only wild fruit and fungi (a fact I mention not in my missives to Florence).

Lately, most locals refuse to barter with us. Their crops are dry and their stores depleted, they say. So we forage. And, luckily, Virgil is adept at fishing. He releases stupefying extracts into the water so that fish may be taken by hand.

"Our time will come," he says.

Rest assured, unlike the natives of Zumbo, we will not eat our own kind.

By water or land, these are perilous trails, Murchison. Our conditions have the makings of a powder keg.

As I said, we will rest here. Otherwise we would be obliged to leave ten of our sick behind. We have had more than three times that number exterminated—speared, arrowed, or clubbed—by the natives, thus far. Others have deserted. So we cannot spare even these sick men.

I must close now. I pray the worst of our ordeals lie behind us, yet fear more are to come.

Yours obediently,

H. R. Huxtable

# LETTER XIII.

*(Addressed to Mrs. H. H. Huxtable,
dated 18 June 1888)*

Dearest Mother—

This day has been spine-tingling from the start.

How are you and venerable Father? Well, I trust. Foraging about for fungi and the like, bearing the weight of copious hardships on my shoulders, England feels so far away now. What I would give for one of your baked dinners! Or even your simple Norman Hash.

As I donned my bark robe in my tent this morn, I happened to examine myself, and my emaciation frightened me. Soon that was not all that did.

Brace yourself, Mother.

For a moment later I heard a flurry of movement—and I faced an African lion.

I knew I should yell, but I could not.

The creature let out an awful roar.

Petrified, I fell back onto my camp-cot. Before I could move, the shaggy beast leaped atop me. Merciless yellow eyes staring me down, it proceeded to lick my face, as if for a taste-test.

Its hot breath blew against me, rank and primal.

My own breath wedged in my throat.

Muffin had said lions kill by breaking a man's neck. They then devour the torso and legs. Crushed under this man-eater, the thought did not cheer me.

Could I free up an arm and pummel the beast, the way my captains routinely had done to each other?

No.

I dared not stir.

I feared to even blink.

As I waited for its piercing canines (if so they are called on a feline) to sink into my flesh and rip me apart, the tent flap ripped open and halted him.

Miss Eaton snapped her whip.

"Git away!"

Tail lashing back and forth, the great cat turned and growled fiercely. She snapped her whip again.

The beast bolted away.

I will be forever grateful to her, though I fear the sight of that creature straddling and licking me has given her ideas.

Now I know what possessed Captain Muffin to abscond: pure terror. Africa is not a friendly place, and here the fickle hand of Death waves me by almost daily.

"Crikey!" I said at last.

Only then did I realise I was trembling, with a hint of giddy happiness that I had survived.

This was my second lion encounter. Henceforth, when we encamp, I shall order the men to install thorn bushes around us for fencing.

For reasons I trust are obvious, I will not say the weather is fine and I wish you were here.

I still remember your motherly words upon my departure: "Dress warm, you'll catch your death." I may catch my death, but it will not be from the cold. I know you are not much for geography, but as it happens Africa is quite hot. Often the heat vibrates in the air.

As for other news, Captain Muffin has deserted, and Captain Fuggleby has met his demise—perhaps just reward for his threatened mutiny.

But let me explicate, without boring you with needless detail. In early June, the man flew into one of his rages. Before long he threatened to flatten me like an oatcake. He was in quite a tizzy. He also spat on one of my walking-shoes.

After this episode, our entire force remained testy. They grumbled and grumbled.

I wondered how best to reinforce my authority. Again I called our group together. It was noon and so hot that nothing stirred. After a variety of impressive poses, under a cobalt-blue sky I delivered a ringing lecture on explorer discipline. Despite my sun helmet, sweat poured down my face.

Virgil translated. Perhaps he fouled up the words, though, because some of the men broke into sniggers. Was it laughter of the nerves? Or were they discomfited to compare themselves to such an unselfish, astute leader?

"I shall care for you as a prudent father cares for his children," I said lastly. "May God be with us all."

Only a few feet away, Fuggleby stroked his ragged beard and muttered through clenched teeth.

"Nay, no more."

With those words, I knew I was on a slope that was getting steeper—and there was no calling a halt.

That eve, I sat in my tent reading up on the rare albino African muskrat. I felt pleasantly full after a dinner of rice and groundnut sauce. Outside, the last hint of daylight had faded to purple and then dissipated in full. The nightjars trilled. As I sipped happily at my tea, a bullet blasted through my tent's canvas. It narrowly missed my head.

This greatly disturbed my relaxation.

Although the fierce temperature had dipped, suddenly I warmed. Here in Africa all sorts of predators came out at dark.

I snatched up my revolver and recruited three loyal askaris for support. Starlight, a sentry-campfire's glow, and our bobbing lanterns cut through the darkness as we hustled towards Fuggleby's tent, primed for a confrontation.

Shortly, I poked my head inside.

"Sir!" I said. "What've you been up to?"

The tent reeked of unwashed clothing. He stepped forward from a velvety black shadow and did not look over-pleased to see me.

After a moment of sulphurous silence, I asked where he had been a few moments before. The rogue feigned a look of surprise and claimed to have been sleeping. He rubbed his bloodshot eyes and yawned theatrically. As usual, he stank of spirits, and his greasy hair was wildly unkempt—there was no telling if it was sleep-mussed or not.

I hissed a curse under my breath.

Yet the truth would not hide: he was shamming. By lantern and touch, we quickly ascertained that his revolver's barrel still felt warm, and fresh-burnt powder showed on his fingers.

When I released his meaty hand, a curtain of hair fell across his face. He flicked it back, then embellished his story.

"Well, now, come to think, it seems…I were dreaming? I, I think I took me a shot at the devil, maybe walking in me sleep."

What fimble-famble!

For a spell all I heard was the rush of insects besieging our lanterns and the tent's canvas. Then came the quick, high laugh of a distant jackal, which seemed an appropriate response to Fuggleby's pathetic lies.

Sick of the man, I scowled at him.

"Perhaps you misjudge me, Captain." I shot a finger into the air. "I must warn you. Librarians do not die easily!"

He is not known to sleep-walk, Mother. And before I left, he further gave himself away with a venomous little smile.

Saved once again by Providence or luck, need I add that I lay under, and not in, my camp-cot afterwards? I saw no reason to change into my nightwear and took repose in even my boots.

My Webley lay close by.

As I lay there, the incident gnawed at me. So did the mosquitoes, despite my netting and the smoke discharging from my smudge pot. Soon the guttural call of howler monkeys added to my disquiet; I could not settle.

After a while I realised that only a goodly slug of Mrs. Winslow's Soothing Syrup could bring me sleep. Oh, how it would linger so pleasantly on my tongue! With one slug, a heavenly calm! I crawled out from under my cot. I lit a candle. Then I lifted the lid of my trunk. Vacant! I slammed the lid shut.

Forty—*forty!*—precious bottles. Gone.

Oh, Fuggleby!

Good God, when did the ruffian accomplish that? Had he acted merely out of spite? Or did he confuse its health-giving properties with the baser spirits he so cowardly indulged in?

My ambrosia, my revitaliser! Words cannot sufficiently describe the blow dealt me by this sinister act.

Early morn, I woke from a fitful, sorry sleep. My mood was dark and brooding. I skipped my morning stand-up wash and instead poked a finger into the rough bullet hole in my tent's canvas. The weight on my shoulders, never light since my arrival on the continent, seemed to double.

"How unsporting," I said, shaking my head.

The debased wretch was out of control.

I found it impossible to suppress my indignation. My hands shook. I rubbed my palms hard against my trousers. Such villainy! Well, if he wanted to push, two could play at that. No mere verbal lashing would end this situation.

I looked around outside. It felt like every bush or tree might hide a crouching figure. But afterwards as I tended to my daily knee bends and arm waving, I knew what must be done.

The next day, Captain Fuggleby was found with a bullet hole much like the one in my tent. He had breathed his last vile breath.

As far as I am concerned, the case is closed. To save the body, one must sometimes hack off a limb.

Fuggleby is gone "where the wicked cease from troubling," as the porters say. And thank heavens, all forty bottles of my restorative tonic lay safe in one of his lockers.

"Found him pistol in hand," I said afterwards to our ragtag caravan. "He's shot himself."

No one seemed specially dismayed.

His burial was a hasty one. Monkeys mocked us from the trees as Lieutenant Potter said a few words, and we left a cross over his grave.

Scoundrel that he had been, I did murmur a prayer for him, then, after a final "Rest in peace, Captain," we marched on.

I wonder yet whatever became of our other captain, Muffin. The man left us in a demented state of mind, Mother. Was he traipsing through the jungle now, conversing animatedly with the monkeys and birds?

More likely, the cannibals ended up with a Muffin on their menu.

Thus, I am without captains.

Yet I have a lieutenant now, and in contrast, this Lieutenant Potter is a joy, Mother—educated and inquisitive, although sassy at times. The man is even titled, he claims, mumbling some impressive-sounding birthright. (He may be embarrassed by his blue-blood heritage.) He dresses like a salty buccaneer, and he gets along well with Miss Eaton, trading scarves and face paint.

A sword swings at his side for flair. He oft taps the porters on the bum with the scabbard's tip in fun, but they do not appear to find it amusing.

He says he dreams constantly of jellied eels and rock candy. While I do not share his tastes, instead dreaming of your pigeon pie and jam roly-poly, there is a drought and general famine in the region and we are all quite hungry. Although this is the rainy season, there is no rain.

While earlier in our mission I would stop and share Bibles with the natives along our path, now I lack both energy and time for spiritual elevation. Mere survival is the only thing on our sun-baked minds, and we must bash on for Fort Bim.

Sometimes I feel we are back in the Stone Age. The other day, before Virgil could even signal me on his bamboo whistle, a savage sprinted out of the bush and thwacked me on the head with a long branch. Thank heavens, he could not even come up with a bona fide club. (Thank heavens also that I had my sun helmet strapped on tightly.)

Potter shot the fellow dead. He is skilled with his silver-in-laid rifle.

When not paddling along in our dugouts, we trudge the riverbank and narrow native paths. We march for hours between hamlets of pole-and-thatch huts. Weakened from the fever, the toil, and our limited diet, we drag ourselves along. At times I totter. I do not think we impress the locals much.

And lately I find our force's mood has gone from recalcitrant and sullen to raw and shaken. It takes effort not to be fed up with everything.

The reality of the situation hit me one evening as I sat with Virgil by a flickering camp-fire.

"This is my expedition!" I snapped. "The men must push harder."

Endless stars pricked through the blue-black sky. The moon shone down brilliantly.

With his usual calm manner, he stared into the flames and considered my statement. We sat without words for a moment. At last, he squeezed his palms together and looked at me.

"We are all working," he said solemnly.

Our eyes clashed.

I said, "I will be damned if—"

"You, me, all."

He pointed to me, then to himself, then spread his arms to indicate the entire camp.

Sobered by his uncommon show of disagreement, for Virgil has always been the one I can rely on for support, I blew out a breath.

"I'm...I'm sorry. Yes, you're right, Virgil—spot-on. Forgive my lapse."

"As my people say, 'Two buttocks cannot avoid the rubbing.'"

A million frogs croaked out from the bush. Our fire crackled, spitting out sparks.

"Indeed." I unhooked my spectacles and wiped the lenses with my handkerchief, then replaced them, pondering his words all the while. "I truly don't want anyone shooting through my tent again."

Occasionally as we approach a village, we shoot off a gun to convey strength. We then drop down onto a straw mat to barter for whatever we can. But often we are treated like unwelcome in-laws.

Recently we found a man bound fast to a pole planted in our path. The poor wretch was dead. Clearly, this was a warning. It appeared we had camped near Umtali, the village of the Iba king, Carambo, and he wanted us to take an alternate route. We obliged. But even on this alternate route, some natives slipped past our sentries and mutilated a carrier.

In contrast, another tribe set fire to their hamlet rather than face us.

The half-charred effigy of me we found in the smoking ruins proved a shock. It was a near dead-ringer, right down to the leopard-printed bark cloth, and eye-glasses fashioned out of trade-wire.

Sweat ran in rivulets down my back as I inspected it, and I swallowed drily.

"Strange."

Though still partially burnt and smouldering, I cut a dashing figure, if I must say so myself. The tiny ivory horns protruding from the wooden helmet were a striking touch.

If we still had the proper apparatus intact, I would have photographed it for you, Mother.

What type of sorcery was this? Was I being worshipped? Or hexed?

In spite of the tropical heat, I shivered. What the figure portended I could not tell.

At times, even my own men do not want to rally behind me.

Recently, we were about to attack a small village to secure needed rations. I found myself well in front of the rest of the column. As I advanced, my rifle at the ready, everyone else apparently stepped backward in unison.

In a way, we attacked and retreated at the same time.

The move thoroughly confused the natives.

I should say it also confused me.

Yet it also gave us a momentary advantage which allowed us to succeed in our raid, and we may try it again in our next skirmish.

If we end up with any remaining rifles, that is—some soldiers have traded theirs for grain. Given the too-common flashes of spears and arrows lately, we are low on cartridges as well.

We have also had unwillingness among the remaining carriers. Demoralised by hunger and suffering, sometimes they turn a deaf ear to our entreaties and refuse their duty. They cite odd taboos: for instance, they say they may not carry loads over fifty pounds, or the Earth will die.

"So it is written," they chant in unison in Kiswahili.

They will not bear banners anymore, either.

"So it is written."

Yet they fail to show me *where* it is written, and one wonders why these taboos are only being mentioned now.

Often I hear them speaking their language in low, intense voices.

One recent day, their murmuring and reluctance reached a new level. We had toiled up to the top of a steep hill. It was the head of two different valleys; further on rose bare-rocked mountaintops. The men had halted, and nothing could induce them to get moving. They stood their ground defiantly.

"Not like look in men's eyes," Virgil said.

Lord knew I was weary myself, but for Jepson's sake, for the mission, we had to keep moving.

After mopping away the sweat from my brow, I gave them all an hour's respite. I also ordered the distribution of extra kolanut biscuits. Afterwards, I stood among them and threw up my arms for attention.

Sisu, the porter headman, said, "Oh my, my brothers—here he goes again."

I thought I heard a slight snort from another of the English-speaking carriers.

Without hesitation, I initiated one of my rousing speeches. This rapidly brought our force to their feet and moving away from me.

My mere authoritative presence had put some snap into them!

"That's right, men," I said. "Carry on! Time you earned your wages."

Our column trudged on.

Dysentery is our enemy, too. For your sake I will skip the horrid details. I do not think the brown water that we must drink on occasion helps in this regard.

As with Miss Eaton, it turns out Virgil makes quite a physician. He dresses and trims up the ulcerous. And he applies cut-root poultices with flair.

"You, fellow, are a wonder," I tell him.

I hope you shall meet him someday, Mother. Along with his knowledge of human nature and medicinal plants is a more than passing knowledge of cookery. A number of his recipes border on the extraordinary. He says even the coiled python can be good eating. Alas, today we shall have to make do with our imitation gruel again.

After crossing a savannah and trudging up endless hills before encamping, we are all knackered. Although I struggle to keep despair—that old curse—away, I will not let indolence rule.

Nor has my skull yet been fashioned into a cannibal drinking cup, for which I give thanks.

The other day, feverish, I thought I saw Ringi's pet chimp in the bush. If you ever meet up with a cannibal, Mother, run in the opposite direction. This much I have learnt.

I must close for now. Once we rest, our caravan of misfits, invalids, and malcontents will continue diving headlong into the unknown.

Yours in the spirit of Christ, your loving son,

Hubert

# LETTER XIV.

*(To Mrs. H. H. Huxtable, dated 27 June 1888)*

Dear Mother—

I had to correspond again: our dear Miss Eaton has met her earthly demise. But I do not want to—I cannot, I will not—believe it.

All the men seem stunned by the loss. Our camp is not the same without her incessant ribald chatter and fag-smoking.

Though the woman claimed herself a founding member of the Christians for Celibacy Society, she was no dainty type. And though I miss her keenly, even I must admit she was obviously not here in Africa to promote celibacy, but perhaps to stamp it out.

How can I be discreet?

She was a rather active woman, Mother.

It turns out she liked animals, too.

(I shall try to be delicate as I relate the details, but please stop and rip this letter up if your heart palpitations come on.)

"I'm a-going off!"

Those were the last words I shall ever hear from Miss Eaton's painted lips, and I feel I shall hear them forever. As always, the woman screeched. (She also sang at times, yet unlike a canary. A dreadful racket, really.)

Virgil followed her into the bush; the rest of the tale is his and I relate it second-hand.

Adaptable as ever, the woman had made herself up in a fantastic head-dress of feathers and beads. Apart from an ivory anklet, she was fully naked, as if stating some formidable truth. Virgil says he was attracted by this costume, but that she said she had no time for him. He followed her, at a short distance, nonetheless. (The man is curious as a cat.) Losing her briefly, apparently he scaled a tall tree to take a sighting. (He is also highly agile.)

He finally spotted her lighting a fire near a great thorn thicket. Since his view was unobstructed, he waited in his perch. From there he witnessed the rest.

"It is hard to tell this," he said afterwards, swallowing.

Soon, she lured in a snorting young rhino (likely it was attracted by the fire).

And then, he swears, the two had congress.

From the general marks on her body, apparently some kind of contact occurred, but I cannot believe Virgil saw what he says he saw. She may have been impaled; afterwards, I could not bring myself to look closely.

Virgil said he almost fell from his tree at the goings-on. Transfixed, he could not tell if her final cries were those of agony—or of ecstasy.

"She died with a smile," they sometimes say, and perhaps she did, too.

As I say, this is a strange land, Mother.

Under an overcast sky in a clearing edged by spiny-looking acacia trees, we paid our last respects. We had laid her out in a frock and cloak, whip at her side. She deserved a carved oaken coffin, bestrewn with floral wreaths, but the best we could do was to wrap her body from head to toe in blue-and-white-striped calico. To prevent the jackals from digging her up, we buried her deeply.

Now, stones bordered the low mound of red earth above her, and the cross at its head read "Sacred to the Memory of Constance Eaton." With a long face, for the two had been fast friends, Lieutenant Potter intoned over her grave to the sounding of a kudu horn.

"I will lift up mine eyes unto the…"

We prayed.

As we did, a great sense of the mystery of life rushed in upon my heart. My sun helmet tucked in one arm, tears streamed down my face.

I wept for her, and all of us.

It was a quiet affair. I almost wished Fuggleby and Muffin were about, simply to liven things up. Miss Eaton had never been one to mope.

Instead, I recited from Isaiah: "Thus saith the Lord, Heaven is my throne, the earth my footstool. Where is the house that ye built unto me? And where is my place of rest?"

I bowed my head, bit my lip, and stood in silence. After a while I looked about at our pitiful group. We were weary men with empty stomachs. And there was to be no woman among us now. Such a grievous blow!

A line from Wergeland came to mind: Death following the happy man like a stern master. Maybe it was as it should be, for her to die and rest here in the wilds of Africa. She was no muffin-walloper, happy to gossip over tea and cakes; the jungle seemed her natural element. Perhaps from here she had found her way to heaven.

I think I loved her, Mother.

(Do not tell Florence this much, please. As things stand now, I do not even have the heart to write her.)

As we ended the service, I turned to Virgil, yet my voice failed me. He stared into the distance, his eyes welling up.

"We will not forget her!" porter headman Sisu said.

They miss her, too, in their own way. She was sort of a strange lioness to them. Curiously enough, they learned to enjoy one of her songs, and would howl with approval when she bellowed "The Ratcatcher's Daughter."

"You know, Virgil," I said at last, "I also enjoyed, well, a dalliance with her."

He frowned in perplexity.

"This word? I do not—"

"Bodily relations. The day she saved me from the lion, we…"

"Of course, I know of this."

"It's best forgotten. Yet when I remember it…"

"On this mission, no secrets."

She had brought us consolation. She had nursed our wounds. With a snap of her whip, she had saved me from that untoward lion—and then later soothed me further than any bottled tonic syrup ever could. And she had helped me stand up to Fuggleby, and to Ringi.

In a way, she was twice the man I am.

And now, though we have her memory to stir us on, my spirits have dipped low.

How do I go on without her? Is it even worth it?

Almost from the beginning our force has been filled with discord: verbal assaults, fisticuffs, defiance of authority, resentments, recriminations. We are now weeks behind schedule. Such setbacks and surprises where life and death are mingled so closely, I have not experienced before, and I find myself besieged by doubts.

Was Miss Hoople right, months ago, when she snorted dismissively about our mission's prospects? I shall never forget how she pinned me with her beady eyes that day. I cannot forget her bitter pronouncement: "Already a sorry excuse for a librarian, now you'll fail as a leader!"

Am I not fit to command this party now? Was I ever fit?

I sometimes used to sign off with a "Hip, hip, hooray," but I will not this day. May the great and good God have mercy on us.

I am simply: your loving son,<br>Hubert

# LETTER XV.

*(Addressed to the Foreign Affairs Editor of*
The London Monitor *and dated 19 July 1888.*
*Written originally on sheets of newsprint.)*

Henry–

How are you, old chap? Jungle greetings to you and all the fellow lodge members. I hope London is getting along well without me. Despite my strange dreams to the contrary, I imagine it is.

We here are getting along—but not specially well.

Our not-so-chaste Miss Eaton has died in a sex act with a rhino. (There, I have said it.) We have left her far behind in body, if not in soul. As I say, life is strange; I miss and regard her more fully now, dead, than when she was alive and kicking.

I am in love with a dead woman.

But enough of that, Henry. (And please forgive the slovenly appearance of this letter. I have not lost my faculties, but I have lost my pen-set. Thus I write with ink made from the juice of

berries on these old newspaper sheets, out of necessity—a fitting substitute considering your profession.) Let it suffice to say that there is unexpected sorrow and pain in this expeditioning.

There is a shortage of paper, too.

Many marches later, we are in the sullen, black Mzim Forest. There is no drought hereabouts.

Up until now, though, it has been a dry, famine-stricken route. Well before reaching the forest, we had abandoned our dugouts, given the lack of rivers. Hunger, that hard master, drove us on through the rugged terrain. Our supply of meat lozenges diminished, and many a day we were forced to get by on a mere biscuit and cupful of gruel. Jettisoning what equipment we could, we trudged along, pierced with hunger pangs and wearing grim looks.

"We must take heart," I told myself.

Some of the men had resorted to taking up their belts a few notches in an effort to relieve the gnawing of their bellies. At least they had belts, I told them. I myself am clothed only in a bark robe and thus without such recourse (the remainder of my clothing having been thieved).

Our force grumbled and complained, and accusations of ration-stealing began to fly. Even Virgil's sunny disposition was tested.

"Troubles no come singly," he said.

Lately, he has acted oddly, donning some of the undergarments found in Miss Eaton's belongings. Ever resourceful, he has tailored them to his own size. Sometimes he runs about in a plum garter belt and mesh stockings below his loincloth. Lieutenant Potter seems to approve.

Perhaps the stress of hunger has altered our minds. At one point we thrilled at the discovery of a game path and fresh excrement. Somewhere nearby was meat! Our excitement lasted for only a short, cruel while—even crafty Virgil could not locate the source.

Instead, we shared again a meal of improvised gruel—water, a cup of flour, condensed milk. How I yearned for a biscuit! What I would have given for a dish of blackcurrant and apple pudding and cream!

Finally, aching with hunger, I broke out my last cans of mutton. These were shared in tiny portions by all. We scooped it greedily into our mouths.

As we moved on, Virgil released a big sigh.

"We will feed the vultures."

I eyed the men staggering along. Some were yellow with fever. All were weary, starving, and heartsick.

"I won't let us fail," I said.

"Chocolate!" Virgil smacked his lips. "That treat we once shared? Some of that I would like."

More than once we forced the local villagers into turning over foodstuffs; more than once they put up a protest. One poor specimen of a chief insisted we need not even bother looking for edibles, since everything that happens to us occurs by permission of the one who watches over us.

We were meant to starve, he seemed to mean.

This is a perverse continent, I think, Henry.

Many of our turbaned Zanzibari carriers maintained an unfriendly profile, too. Faces etched with fear and hunger, they deserted and died on us without warning. This was a distressing trend. "So it is written!" they would tell me, I imagine, it being their favourite refrain.

A black cloud seemed to hang over us. Essential supplies began to disappear. Before long we were losing goods and foragers right and left.

Given our desperation, I sent out a messenger. His orders were to head for the nearest, though distant, trading station. He carried a handwritten note requesting help and supplies. He was our only hope.

Some men could not stand unaided and had to be helped along by others. If attacked while so weakened, we were doomed.

"We must survive this day," I said routinely to all.

Our numbers diminished. And some who remained began to exhibit dangerous looks. One day a bitter fight broke out over where to encamp, until I silenced the men and made the site selection myself, feigning a show of confidence. Inwardly, with scant success I tried to fight off my growing fear that our expedition might truly fail.

Would we be forced to turn cannibals ourselves? Would any of us survive to reach beleaguered Fort Bim? Was this all a testament to my folly?

When we came across our messenger, my heart dropped. Dead.

Pierced with arrows.

Flies buzzed all about.

Soon, even Virgil could not locate more tubers or fruits, and it was a trial to think about anything but food. A mounting desperation began to infect us. All of us perhaps a trifle off our heads, we savoured what insects we could catch.

At last, Virgil and I wheezed to a stop and took shade under a flat-topped acacia tree. A flock of vultures perched in the nearby canopy. Their pink heads were grotesque. They roosted there like an evil omen, waiting.

I was tired. Tired of fighting, tired of pushing on, tired of this continent.

I looked down. My boots were toe-sprung, rudely patched. My feet were dead things. The steamy air pressed against us as I ran my hand over my sweaty face and breathed out a sigh of utter resignation.

We were doomed.

"We can't go on. I'm sorry, I've…I did all…Folly. This is folly."

"You cannot take blame."

"Can't I?"

He shook his head.

"We come so far, Mr. Huxtable. We must go on."

Softly, he began to chant. Though I could not fathom the words, his song was strangely heartening, and I found myself beginning to rally.

"Right," I said at last.

Virgil had his wits yet, and I thanked God for his steady counsel. Though all looked bleak, we could not simply give up. It was time for a last desperate attempt.

Forward.

One step, two steps. My right foot throbbed so, I could scarcely move. My legs shook like a new-born fawn's.

"If we die," I said to the men, "we'll die walking."

I had to give this everything I had. Let the bloody vultures starve. Every step brought us closer to Fort Bim.

Eventually we reached the Mzim Forest. When we located bananas at the jungle's outskirts, our feeble crew managed a cheer. It was as if a hand had reached out to pull us from the abyss.

Heavens, how we would eat!

Excitedly, ravenously, we gorged ourselves on fruit. We stopped only when we grew sick.

Now that starvation seemed less likely, a new difficulty arose: the jungle was terrible, a teeming, impenetrable hothouse. Little light filtered through the canopy. Hour after hour we faced unbroken greenness—leafy tangled branches, roots, and vines. Loaded down with fruit, we hacked away at the thick under-growth.

About midday, our newly determined party halted at my command. The heat beat in on us, and we all needed water.

Covered in a slick of sweat and in search of a spring or stream of some sort, I stepped into a tiny clearing.

Right away a curious sinking feeling overcame me, Henry. As soon as I had put my foot down, I felt a sucking motion below it.

In a moment my right leg disappeared up to the knee.

I stuck fast in a quagmire of quicksand, with no men about able—or willing—to pull me to safety. I felt a cold, cramping fear.

Desperately, I grasped at a low-lying branch. But the branch suddenly twisted about my arm: a pernicious python!

"Bugger."

The scaly, thick snake seemed to grin at me. Pythons, I remembered reading, operate via constriction. Would it grab hold of something and pull me out, my deliverer?

This seemed a dangerous outcome to bank on, so I managed to jerk my arm free, but doing so made me sink further in the morass.

Dash my wig!

Was I doomed?

At that moment, Virgil raced up and thrust a broken tree-limb towards me.

"Grab tight!"

With a mighty effort on both our parts, he pulled me out of the sand, where we both lay, gulping in air.

"Jolly good," I said at last.

I have not sighted the rare albino African muskrat—but I have stared the wild python in its beady eye and lived to tell of it, Henry.

We continued our way into the jungle's gloomy, moist bosom. Ankle-deep in mud and water, we chopped at the rank vegetation. The gnats rose in great black clouds. Huge balls of mud formed round our feet: yellow mud, black mud, brown mud. In the cheerless twilight, we kept our eyes open for other coiling creepers and the fall of rotten trees.

"Marching into roadless jungle?" Virgil said. "This you get."

I did not remind him this route was his idea in the first place.

"Just keep going!" I said.

When the jungle thickened even further, we tore, scrambled, and crawled through it. Everything smelled of decomposition. Thorns slashed our arms and faces; our skin swelled and itched from insect bites. After being stung or bitten by something I did not see, one of my knees reddened, and soon it released foul matter, so that the fluid saturated my stocking. Others suffered eyelids swollen from ticks.

Once, Virgil had called this region home, but now he is an outsider looking in. We sensed his people watching. Would they welcome us? Or would they try to repel our paltry force with poisoned darts and traps? I prayed for the former.

Sinking in muck-holes and the occasional elephant track, slipping on water-slicked rocks and tripping over fallen trees, I wished we could swing from the dense foliage roof by manner of hanging vines, as the monkeys do. De-evolution, as it were.

The hanging mosses and branches glistened with dew and a steady mist; I thought we should never dry out. The sweet-sour odour of jungle rot wafted off our clothes.

Our column even clashed with a colony of furious ants. We lost. After hastily leaving the area, we stopped and stripped off our garments to pluck them from our sweaty flesh. These little devils are known to devour a rifle stock overnight.

"My people are not far," Virgil said the next day.

"Not far?" I said. "Not far? You've been saying that for—"

"Few days more."

This time he proved to be correct: on 15 July we met his tribe. An entire diminutive, bushy-browed party loomed suddenly out of a dense fog, blowguns in hand. Keeping a careful distance, they looked up at us as if we were from another planet.

We stood there, knackered, hoping for welcome that, if not warm, would at least not require us to defend ourselves.

"Kemla!" they soon began to cry, gladly. "Kemla!"

They were overcome to see Kemla (their name for Virgil), one of their own, in such costume and company. Likely, they looked at our rag-clothed and scratched-up bodies and pitied us, too, for some of the bolder little fellows then rushed in to clap us on the backs, smiling and laughing.

Finally finding his voice, Virgil drew his people into a circle. He then regaled them with tales of our exploits, and those of his own life since his leave-taking.

It has been like "Old Home Week" since then.

A series of whistle calls announced our approach as Virgil's tribe led us through the forest that day to meet the others. Before long, we held a gala bush party. In a copse dripping with humidity, we swung our axes and billhooks to enlarge a clearing. Each blow left the chopper drenched with a shower-bath. A falling tree almost cracked Lieutenant Potter on the head. A rotten branch just cleared his nose.

That night, despite the insects and hothouse atmosphere, we managed to have a jolly good time. Even a spell of torrential rain could not dampen our spirits.

Squatting on our heels, we feasted on endless bowls of mushrooms, berries, nuts, wild beans, and charred elephant meat. The askaris finally let out their belts. And we drank pombe, too. As bananas boiled for our dessert, I thought it an opportune moment to present the courteous headman, Ikan, with a cuckoo-clock, and did so with pomp and circumstance. (True, the clock had stopped working. But, then again, what need do the Wambutti have for telling time?) Ikan appeared greatly honoured. His sinewy arms adorned with elephant-skin bands, he passed the timepiece around to his tribe with a beaming smile.

At first, some of Virgil's kin had barely looked into our eyes, but the drinking helped in this regard. So did the cannabis the Zanzibaris pulled out. Soon even a few of the shyer Wambutti admired my decorated bark robe and marvelled at my cracked spectacles.

Despite the smoke from the wet fires, and the rain and mist, we entertained ourselves with story and libation for hours. The night air turned deliciously cool. As I drank and smoked, I could not tell myself nothing was right anymore—here we sat in the maw of the jungle, feasting with generous-hearted dwarfs.

With half-mast eyes, Virgil kept busy in translating back and forth, back and forth. The Wambutti marvelled at our tales of Zumbo, the filed teeth and elaborate hairdos of the cannibals therein, and so on.

Waxing nostalgic, I wished Miss Eaton could have been there, munching on plantains with the rest of us.

"I keep expecting her to show up among us," I finally said to Virgil.

He touched his heart with his hand.

"I miss her also."

My spectacles misted repeatedly, and I squinted through the mingled smoke of damp wood and sweet cannabis. Yet I did not care. It was such a relief to take repose, full of food and drink, surrounded by friends. Could we not just stay on with these gentle, generous people?

Though we were tired, we were eventually cajoled into dancing. Despite Miss Eaton's absence, the occasion still had a certain romance. There we were, nearly naked, forming a large circle around the fire. We waved clubs, battle-axes, and the cuckoo-clock even, and stamped one foot, then the other.

Will you think less of me if I say I gave myself up to the moment, Henry?

The last of my worries dissipated. Well into my cups with the pombe and cannabis, I laughed in delight as we shuffled, stomped, and howled, a regular chorus-line.

Alas, in the morning, the dance marathon was but a brief blur in my memory, greatly overshadowed by my throbbing skull. I thought I might die, suffering the rebuke of Providence in my savage hut.

When at last I eased my clouded head outside, I sighted genuine black clouds—those of an imminent set-in rain—so I confined myself to my hut for the day.

Virgil spent his day undercover, too, with some friendly belles.

The following morn, interested in learning about the tribe's hunting skills (for a possible future lodge meeting presentation), I accompanied them on a foray into the bush.

There I was on an actual elephant hunt, Henry!

For a while, we followed a large fresh track. Headman Ikan finally gestured for silence. We heard the shuffle of giant feet and the scraping of hide against a tree.

As the bushes cracked about us, I held my breath.

The immense beast passed by and fed here and there on palm nuts.

We followed. Courageous Ikan ran up and leaped on the creature's moving leg. He struck with his large knife to sever its hind-foot tendon before sprinting off with a triumphant holler.

"I would not try this," I told myself.

The great beast began to limp, and eventually fell, to be swarmed and killed by the rest of the party.

(I have rendered the scene with my watercolour paints. I must say the results are pleasing.)

As we feasted again, sitting on dropped tree trunks, though, it hit me: what were we bloody doing? Jepson needed us!

Our respite with the Wambutti was a godsend; even for a short while, it had been restorative to feel happy and safe. Yet this was no time to lose my wits or be enslaved by creature comforts: the Mahdist hordes might be advancing on Fort Bim even as we sat.

I put down my wooden platter of food. The canopy teemed with parrots, all making a rather pleasant cacophony. A faint mist fell, coating us with a fine moisture.

"The clock's ticking," I said to Virgil and my other nearby men. "We cannot linger!"

I stood. The others looked at me expectantly. Raising my hands high above my head, I called for quiet.

"On the morrow, we'll cut a road, get cracking." Low groans rose from the men. "We've work to do! We must bash on. Honour and glory beckon!"

Lieutenant Potter and I exchanged a glance, and he nodded in support.

"Jolly good!" he said.

"Indeed."

"Huzzah!"

"For the Queen," I said.

"And Country."

"Well done."

"Quite so."

Virgil gave a sharp sigh, but the look on his face was resigned.

Fort Bim is not far away; if I reckon right, we have but 200 miles to go. Or perhaps 300. We are off our schedule, and an occasional break for afternoon tea may have to be sacrificed. We must resume our perilous quest.

I must bid you adieu, Henry. I am running low on berries; Virgil has been eating them up as I write.

God be with you, if not always with us.

Yours humbly,<br>H. R. Huxtable

# LETTER XVI.



Gentlemen (and Percival Blowden, to whom the appellation does not apply) —

I am overjoyed to report that—despite my often vague sense of direction—our journeying has finally come to an end.

Huzzah!

Still, I do have something awkward to admit:

It seems I have killed Jepson.

Perhaps I should preface that statement? Allow me to go back.

Nearly three weeks ago, as we prepared to take our leave of Virgil's people, our Zanzibari's headman, Sisu, had asked me, "You know of where you are going?"

"It's a bit puzzling, that," I said, donning my helmet, "but yes. Largely. Yes."

Reinvigorated by our respite and spurred on by Virgil and two new Wambutti recruits eager for adventure, before long we left the dank Mzim jungle behind.

We stepped outside it to blue sky, plains, and meadows.

Heavens alive! If I had been carrying a bundle, I would have thrown it down.

We scampered forward to grasp at the grass, laughing and hollering through our pale cheeks.

No more jungle! No more bloated spiders, insects, or serpents masquerading as lianas! The humidity immediately lessened, and I looked forward to having dry feet again.

Unfortunately the grass did not last, and the terrain soon became parched and bare. Still, our spirits were good, since at the very least we were not being assailed by hostile tribes, and we knew our tribulation-filled march neared its end (and my feet did indeed dry out).

Almost a week ago, our forty-four-man caravan crossed a vast belt of desert land. Mica glittered in the soil, and the area looked desolate as the moon. Brown and white spikes of rock rose in the distance.

Under the sun's full wrath, we marched past dark sandstone outcroppings. Then, as we trudged across yet another dried river-bed, it happened: although my eyes burned with the heat, I spotted an apparent cattle track.

"Over there! Is that…?"

Were we actually close to Fort Bim at last?

I called for haste.

"Keep it going, men. Come on! Move! Left, right, left, right, and the devil take the laggards."

Red dust puffed up around our quickening feet.

Soon, we sighted the dun-coloured mud walls of what appeared to be a fort.

Touched by the heat, I swigged from my canteen, but it was empty. My throat was swollen from the lack of water. Under the blue sky, the flat land shimmered. The dust in the air created a slight haze, so I screwed up my eyes to see better. Was this a mirage? Yet the others convinced me this oasis in the howling desert was real.

The sight fairly took our remaining breath away. A rush of triumph built in me, and I felt cheerful as a schoolboy at the end of term. An actual fort—and our final destination!

Spontaneous cheers arose as I laid a hand on Virgil's shoulder. He had been the glue of this mission, without whom we would not have survived.

"By George, we've done it," I said. "*You've* done it, my stalwart friend."

He offered me a cracking salute.

"It has been honour. An honour."

The Jepson Relief Expedition had arrived.

I turned and acknowledged the entire remainder of our force.

"We've done it, men!" I felt a rush of affection. "You've all been brilliant."

Virgil beamed.

"This is good, Mr. Huxtable."

We laughed with giddy pleasure. Lieutenant Potter bussed me on the cheek. Sisu called out with appreciation to the other Zanzibaris, and they shouted what I assumed to be huzzahs.

A part of me tried to soak up the moment, to freeze time. There would be no more discomfort, no more danger. No more death.

It was over.

As we approached the fort, I found myself rejoicing in the thumps of my feet on the baked earth. I imagined Jepson and his men dropping to their knees in gratitude at our arrival. Animated faces would cheer and whistle.

No kudu's horn or bell, though, sounded from within the looming walls. My joy faded. I wiped my brow against the heat, and a case of nerves overwhelmed me. Had something dreadful happened? Would we be met with open arms—or firearms? Had they been overrun? Would we have to lay siege? (As a man trained primarily in the library sciences, my knowledge of sieges was limited.)

Or perhaps death had overtaken the fort's inhabitants?

Were we simply too late?

Lieutenant Potter squinted in concern.

"Good God, something's dodgy here."

Virgil handed me my shotgun, and I cleared my throat.

"All right then, men. Courage. For Queen and Country!"

I felt dizzy—yet I stepped forward. My men followed behind me in proper form, trusty rifles in arm.

The fort entrance swung open at our touch. Knots in our throats, we stepped inside. The inner courtyard and mud thatched-roof buildings lacked signs of any troops—or anyone else, for that matter.

I hallooed.

No-one showed.

Spooked, by accident I discharged my shotgun, but there was still no response from within the fort. We might have blown up the powder magazine without registering complaint.

As we crept forward, muscles tensed, a sole camel and a pack of dogs eyed us curiously. Yet there were no humans.

It was eerie, gentlemen.

What in God's name had happened? Had they all been killed by plague or carried off by Arabs?

The lump in my throat would not go away.

We passed a cart loaded with barrels, stacked watermelons, and hen-coops. Suddenly, Potter gestured and raised his silver-inlaid rifle, but did not shoot. Following his finger, I turned—and was nearly knocked down by a wispy-bearded man in a white turban and emerald robe running toward us, yelling.

"Malonda! Malonda!" (According to Virgil: "Things for sale!")

I pulled him aside to his impromptu market in order to question him, and Virgil followed to translate.

After the bloke's third attempt to hand me a melon, I said shortly, "We aren't here to shop, you bloody fool—we've come for Jepson!"

(But some of the men—perhaps to embarrass me, once again—actually did interrupt and try to barter for melons.)

"What happened here?" I was finally able to ask the man.

His eyes bulged as he explained that we had come in the midst of a week-long drunken company orgy. It seemed Fort Bim was slouching towards debauchery. Lately, the trader went on to say, Jepson had also tortured and enslaved many of the locals.

"Commander is—ha!"

The vendor threw up his hands in despair.

Apparently Jepson was off his head.

"Hyah Barak-Allah!" ("Go, with the blessing of God!") the man said at last, encouraging us to find out for ourselves.

And, of course, an Englishman does not run.

Under the circumstances, overpowering the snoring guards and securing the garrison proved easy, which was fortunate, given our condition. Supposedly to the north roamed the Mahdi's hordes, to the south the wild Utangans. Yet there were no enemies in sight here. The rectangular fort and its stores of weapons proved ours by nightfall.

But it was Jepson I longed to see.

How do I explain?

After everything we had been through, I felt as if he were my fate.

That evening I finally met him. Having been informed in the afternoon that he needed time to sober up, I had waited. Meanwhile, I had located some European-style clothing and restored myself to a more civilised appearance, though I felt a marked sadness at relinquishing my woven-bark garment.

I had also taken the opportunity to partake of Mrs. Winslow's Soothing Syrup. Just seeing the embossed silver-and-gold label began to settle me. I took a goodly slug. Then another.

Carry on, I told myself as I readied to meet Jepson. You are no yellow-belly.

As I stepped into his second-storey chambers, a disagreeable odour assailed me. Was it some odd local incense? It stank like the foul depths of hell, whatever it was. I pinched my nose between my thumb and fingers before proceeding. The room was gloomy, heavy-curtained. In one corner a candle flickered next to a statue of the Virgin. Flies buzzed about.

Jepson loomed in the dark. After releasing my nose and adjusting a tad to the stench, but trying to breathe through my mouth, I cleared my throat.

"Sir, I am Hubert Reginald Huxtable, Commander of the Royal Order of the Muskrat Relief Expedition, and we've come to see you safely back to civilisation," I said. "How do you do, Governour Jepson?"

I hesitated at the doorway.

Bothered by the silence and bitter smell, I spoke again.

"'Look here, chap, we were told you were beset by slavers and marauders. My men and I have marched countless miles to save you. We suffered greatly. But we're here, finally. We're here. And yet there—there seems to be no local threat."

Stirring from the Stygian blackness, he spoke at last in a deep voice.

"Too late, Huxtable. You're too late."

He sounded a touch sozzled still. From his shadow, he seemed a stout, even formidable figure.

Something faraway also registered in his voice.

"Are you i-ill, sir?" I said.

He shuffled into the light, startling me. My eyes widened. Good God!

A hideous case of leprosy disfigured his face and limbs.

His body was decaying like rank vegetation. His skin looked thick and bubbly here, curiously smooth there. His nose resembled a grotesque lobster claw. My own skin grew cold with shock. Gasping for breath, I thought I should faint from the stench—and the sight.

He gave me a piteous grin.

"Seen enough? Now get your stupid bloody face out of here."

Despite his impolite words, I did not leave. Though frightened of him, I could not move.

I knew my own face showed strain.

"A shilling for your thoughts," I said at last.

He was made up in Arab mufti, I should add, which included a turban and embroidered dressing gown. (The Arab influence is strong here.) A monocle was embedded in the folds of his leprous face.

"Tell me," he said, "what is justice?"

At the same time, he extended—to my shock—the misshapen remainder of his right hand.

As a librarian, I well knew the definition of that word: "justice." Yet I did not think it was the answer he wanted. And to touch him? Of course I feared catching his hideous disease. Still, somehow I could not resist.

I was spellbound.

Africa has got me again, I thought—and we shook, hand and stump.

Even now the hackles rise on my neck as does the gorge in my throat at the remembrance.

We then sat in high-backed chairs before a small table and shared bowls of piping hot victuals, Jepson employing his good, though scaly, hand as we ate, and me trying to ignore the odour. The mangoes tasted wonderful, although the custard was burnt. Yet it soon appeared that sharing this meal was not to be a peace-making—far from it.

"Lord paramount of the area, I've made myself," he said. "Yes, I'm ill. And, yes, I used more than…light force here." He paused, as if deliberating. "Yet the entirety of this region is mine."

I was unsure whether to believe him. Still, I listened attentively, fascinated by both his moral and physical decay. I also had no other plans for the evening, nor for the rest of my life, I realised as I savoured my strong black tea. Perhaps I imagined it, but I think part of his ear fell off as I responded.

"Many good men—and one great woman—died on our venture here, sir. We fought, we starved, we suffered torment beyond recounting. We pushed on through bloody forests, swamps, and the rigours of the climate. I endured attacks by lions, rhinos, and a libidinous female. I outwitted cannibals! Some underestimated me—"

He gave a mocking laugh.

"No surprise."

I narrowed my eyes and finished coldly, "—but they are no threat now. Or dead."

With his stump, he wiped the grease from his chin. He then made a scoffing sound.

"Don't you see? Like I wrote you, you bloody idiot, we never needed rescue!"

As I shook my head, he surmised there had been a mix-up in despatches, confusing his fort with another one much further south. After quaffing more of the pombe he had been drinking throughout our repast, he flapped his left hand, which still had most of its fingers, in a gesture of utter dismissal.

"All's quite in order here, as you can see. Go home, Huxtable."

As he had been speaking, my anger had grown.

Now my mouth tightened as I said, "What rubbish, what fimble-famble! Poppycock, I say!"

He lied, gentlemen. He told a scabby lie. As we well know, there was no confusion about the forts in the information we had received—the information that had driven our entire rescue expedition.

This was a disappointment indeed.

My heart rapped at my rib cage as I recalled the venomous note he had sent me. I thought, too, of his crimes here, and his utter ingratitude. And I found myself lathering into a righteous fury.

I thrust out my noble chest.

"I do not like your tone. Nor do I believe your flimsy explanation. Mistaken despatches? You take me for a fool, sir?"

The question hung in the air.

"Good God, Jepson. I don't mean to sound ungenerous, but what you have done here is…barbaric! I fear that you, sir, you… are a lost soul."

It was dark, and he was well into his cups as we shot up from our seats and went at it hammer and tongs; there was plain speaking on both sides. His gestures became increasingly violent.

After minutes of this, his raven-hard eyes virtually exploding with hate, his voice shrill, he shouted, "Bugger off!" and slapped me in the face.

This madman was making our mission appear foolish, gross—something to be expectorated into a spittoon. I thought of our losses on the journey: not just Miss Eaton and the treacherous Fuggleby, but all the porters and soldiers who had given their lives to come to the fort's aid.

I rubbed my palms hard against my trousers. I was no weakling; I was Hubert Reginald Huxtable, Mender of Books and Conqueror of Jungles.

"You have the impudence to lay hand on me!" I said.

I briefly wondered if there were proper etiquette for being attacked by an insane leper, then decided I cared not and grabbed the collar of his dressing-gown.

He grasped me about the waist. We stumbled against a towering cupboard that threatened to topple over on us, then against the table. I broke free of his clenching arm and swung with all my force at his leprous jaw.

He staggered back, towards the balcony.

I planted two hammer-like blows into his ribs. He breathed hoarsely, the rancid smell wafting over me, as I grabbed him by the neck and seat of his trousers.

For a moment I was stilled by a fierce perplexity: was I going to kill the bloke we had sacrificed so much to save?

Bloody hell.

Yes.

I was.

"Sir," I said, "I bid you goodbye," and I thrust him off the balcony.

He landed below with a squashy thud.

Afterwards, lantern in hand, the darkness all around us, I squatted over his limp body. Blood ran from the corners of his mouth. Already sorely lacking in good looks before his fall, he looked very much a mess after it.

"Who's the blockheaded ninny now?" I said at last. "Damn you, Jepson. Damn you!"

It appears I am a man of many parts. Yet I suppose this was a poor sort of rescue.

The next day, I informed the others.

"Everything went contrary to what I expected," I said lastly, and they appeared to understand.

With his demise, I am now the post commander. Save Jepson? Alas, he was long gone before ever we left England. Reportedly he engaged in every possible vice here, including the ivory and slave trade. We hear talk of severed hands and slaughtered natives. (Please include these pertinent facts in the committee's final report, Murchison.)

Though Jepson brought Fort Bim to an utterly debauched state, due to its location it has succeeded as a trading station nonetheless. His small strongbox of accumulated gold pieces will prove useful. Given the abundance of livestock, imported food, and other luxuries, no-one in our force is inclined to march away.

We shall stay.

Worry not, for we will stay vigilant against the Mahdi. Lieutenant Potter and his companion, Dovey, routinely take to the mud-brick ramparts with our telescope to search the heat haze for signs of his forces.

Yet from what I have seen thus far, the local Mohammedans are kind and generous. It makes one wonder just who the villains truly are. Cannibals, Arabs, Europeans—I suppose at heart we are all fellow humans.

Perhaps our arrival marks a positive turning point for British Central Africa. For now, I have inherited spacious quarters and a charming harem. They seem to enjoy our morning group knee bends and arm waving.

"Yes, ladies!" I say to them, with an occasional touch to correct their form. "Bend low, and then up—let us circulate our blood!"

They titter at times, yet they have surely enlivened my daily routine, not to mention my nights.

In accordance with Miss Eaton's views, I do not hold these nubile women against their will. They are free to make their own choices, and those who stay will be well compensated and cared-for.

There is a certain blueness to the sky here which is wholly unlike what one sees in England. The night sky is rich with stars. Under a canopy of them the other night, I marvelled at the course my life has taken. It is the strangest miracle. Or perhaps it was all meant to be.

At least that is what our new addition, the long-absent Captain Muffin, tells me.

I suppose I should explain that, too.

Two days after our arrival, Virgil burst into my chambers, eyes lit up.

"Captain Muffin—he is back!"

I stared at him in astonishment.

"What! Here? How did—"

"I do not know. He rests."

I dropped the papers in my hand.

"Even more strange," Virgil continued, "when I offer him pombe, he say, 'No!'"

"Good God!" I said.

Later in my chambers, Muffin told us his story.

After his departure from our force, apparently an Arab party had carried him off to the desert. Eventually they discarded him, due to his constant carping and shouting. They could not stand him, either, I gather. Disheartened and penniless, with few options, he determined to find his way to Fort Bim on his own.

"What a bloody journey to get here!" he said at last. He had a scabby wound on his brow and every visible inch of his skin was sun-scorched. He wore still his torn and patched suit. "God, I grew a-tired of all that desert. How I wanted some gin! Hurt me bad at first, strong bad. Then all I wanted was—water." He sighed. "All that sand, sand, sand—"

I said, "I understand, Captain."

"—and more bloody sand. So much sand—"

"All right, all right." I pictured him liquored to the gills and staggering about, and picking fights, as he used to, and thought for a heartbeat. "As for us, you must admit your past actions have not inspired a great deal of trust."

"Must confess—don't recall most of those days. Yet I do apologise. Upon my soul, I apologise."

To be fair, he had fought gallantly against the cannibals of the Baseko tribe. And before my parley at Zumbo, had he not earnestly wished me good fortune?

So before long I said, "Then we shall let old quarrels be bygone."

I offered him my hand, which he shook with every appearance of gratitude.

I take his return to our troop as a fortuitous sign. He has gone through the eye of madness and come out the other side. And he has escaped the lure of the bottle.

I have set up him, Virgil, and the other Wambutti recruits in their own large hut. Virgil is quite the sight lately, in his newly tailored white cotton drill suit and neat red fez. Muffin says that the three Wambutti do not take up much space, and all is fine with them. Who knows? Someday he may even shave and comb his unruly vertical hair.

There is a picturesque—dare I say erotic?—element to this place. Also, I find I rather like the feel of a garrison between me and all else right now. As Muffin mumbled to me yesterday, "I ain't crazy, chap, I'm just withdrawing from the world."

After all our adventure, this fort life may prove tedious. And, after all our adventure, that is fine with me. Presently, I am sound of vital organs and limbs. I am sufficiently fed, watered, and housed. Due to the cracks in my glasses, my eyes have gone slightly crossed, but apparently among the desert tribes here, slightly crossed eyes are held in great esteem. Partly shaved, I am resplendent in mutton chops. I have had epaulettes stitched onto my jackets, and even my sleepwear.

"Our time has come," Virgil says.

Muffin agrees.

Life is not always easy—for most, it is no dance on roses. I suppose, though, we must always travel in hope. At the moment I am filled with a queer sense of completion.

This day I purchased from a trader a worn, ancient text. Although in places the original paper has broken down, new bits have been fastened in place. Its fine script is illuminated with gold-leaf droplets, and the cover appears to be skin of goat. It gave me great pleasure to run my hands over this volume. And as I admired it, I had an illumination myself.

We do not require more troops or weapons. But could you arrange the future transport of trunks replete with books? Treatises on logic, astronomy, and medicine? And—only to balance the variety, of course—some illustrated volumes celebrating the sensual?

If we are to remain civilised here, we must have a library.

Should we feel the call of exploration, we have rumour of a sizeable cavern somewhere nearby. Inside an entrance hidden by boulders, it is said to be filled with uncut jewels and gold to an extent greater than that possessed by kings. I find the idea of such treasure difficult to abandon. Muffin and I may find it yet. Potter would fancy some diamonds himself, I think.

But as for staying close to Mother Nature, next time you see her, give her my best. I will submit to no more dense bush or animal attacks.

Presently, I am distracted by the sweet aroma of roasting goat. Even more pleasantly, gentlemen, Fatima is waiting. There is witchcraft on her lips, an abyss of delight within her gaze.

We shall play Chinese checkers. Perhaps smoke some cannabis.

"I feel good," I will tell her. "I feel bloody great."

Then, who knows? As Miss Eaton once said, "Life's meant to include some fun."

Yours from deepest Africa,

H. R. Huxtable,

Commander and Future Librarian of Fort Bim

# ACKNOWLEDGEMENTS

A big thanks to Ryder Author Resources. Huzzah! And to J. S. Keltie's Victorian-era "Letters of Stanley" for the initial inspiration.

# AFTERWORD

My sincere thanks to you for reading and taking this journey with H. R. Huxtable, Virgil, Miss Eaton, and me. If you're moved to leave a review on Goodreads or pretty much anywhere else, your efforts would be greatly appreciated. No problem, if it's not your thing. I hope you enjoyed the story, because that's what matters most.